Michael R. Davidson

Also by Michael R. Davidson

Harry's Rules

Eye for an Eye

Incubus

The Incubus Vendetta

The Inquisitor and the Maiden

Retribution

Krystal

The Dove

The Dead Lawyer

Buy Another Day

With Kseniya Kirillova

In the Shadow of Mordor

Successor

In the development of this novel the author was inspired in part by actual events. Having made this clarification it is important to emphasize the fact that this is a work of fiction and the situations described, as well as the characters and their actions are totally imaginary.

Michael R. Davidson

SPILLED BLOOD

MRD Enterprises, Inc.
PO BOX 1000
Mount Jackson, VA 22844
mrdenter@shentel.net

Library of Congress Control Number: TXu 2-166-101

ISBN-13: 978-0-578-58745-5
ISBN-10: 0-578-58745-9

Contact author at info@michaelrdavidson.com

Cover by Rena Hoberman
http://www.coverquill.com

Printed and bound in the United States of America.

First printing 2019

Miami Last Year

"I think I'm gonna quit."

"Hmmm?" Ray Velazquez rolled lazily onto his side to face her. "Am I that bad in bed?"

She whacked the side of his head. "I'm not going to quit THAT. I mean Arlington."

He propped his head in one hand, definitely listening now. "Really?"

Outside Ray's bedroom window the mid-morning Miami sun was beginning to do battle with the city's air-conditioning units. They'd enjoyed a late night on South Beach, and neither felt guilty for lazing in bed on a Saturday morning. "Really," she repeated. "I've been thinking about it for a long time."

"Do I have anything to do with it?"

"Yeah, but that's not the only reason."

"Care to elaborate?"

"It's just that I'm not happy there anymore. There's a stench around Washington that I can't get out of my nostrils."

"It's really that bad?"

"I can't tell you." But she wished she could.

"OK, let's say you quit. What would you do?"

"I haven't decided."

"You could move down here. I know Dade County would hire you immediately. In fact, I can guarantee it."

"I dunno. Moving from one police department to another doesn't seem so attractive."

She read the disappointment on his face and quickly added, "But I do like Miami."

This cheered him. "So what are you thinking of

i

doing?"

"I've had an interesting job offer."

He raised his eyebrows and waited.

"I could spend more time down here, maybe even move here permanently."

The fact was that Robert Strachey had decided to set up a private security and investigation business, and he wanted her to be part of it at a salary three times what Arlington County paid. It would mean a huge change from the existence she'd known most of her adult life.

She was considering the offer seriously ...

SPILLED BLOOD

Michael R. Davidson

CHAPTER 1

It was one of those perfect days in early summer. The sun was high in an unblemished blue sky but had not yet stoked its furnaces to produce the higher temperatures of mid-summer. Jim Stevens and his buddies from high school were gathered on one of the fields at Park Road Park for a pick-up softball game.

Jim would be a senior the following year, and baseball was his game. He'd settle for softball today because they didn't have the right safety equipment for hardball, and, besides they hadn't found enough guys to make up two full teams. So, it was six men on a side. One guy would have to cover shortstop and third base, leaving only two outfielders who had to be able to move fast.

At the top of the third inning, Jim was coming to bat. He'd singled in the first inning and was confident he could smack the slow-moving softball over the outfielders' heads. The pitcher was preparing to throw when they heard it.

A loud report from the direction of the pond on the other side of the park, followed by three more. Had there been a faint scream? Everyone froze. "Geez, were those gunshots?" asked the pitcher.

The first baseman, Greg Collins, also a senior, was a hunter and knew the sound of a firearm when he heard it. "It sure as hell was," he said.

They all stood in indecision for a moment, looking at one another, before Greg yelled, "Let's get over there."

"What if it's some crazy guy with a gun?" asked

one of the boys.

"We can't just stand here," said Greg. "I'm going over there."

He took a few steps in the direction of the shots, at first tentatively, and then as his determination rose, broke into a trot.

Gloves and bats left behind on the ground the rest followed him toward the pond that was separated from the field by a thin line of trees and a small shed used by park maintenance to store equipment. Emerging onto the paved path that circled the pond they were attracted by a keening wail from the far end where they could see people lying motionless on the ground. No one else could be seen.

"Christ," exclaimed Jim, "do you see that?"

Collectively conscious that they were walking into a mass shooting, the boys hesitated, casting wild-eyed glances at one another wondering if a maniac with a gun might be heading toward them. But there was no one in sight, and the high-pitched, hysterical cries continued to shatter the air. Afterwards, they could not recall how long they stood there in indecision and fear, but finally Greg ran down the path toward the people on the ground, and the others again followed.

They arrived in a group and drew up sharply, gaping at the scene of carnage. Two people, a man and a woman, were sprawled near a picnic blanket spread on the verge of the pond with food and containers scattered on the ground around them. A short distance away on the path a man wearing cycling gear lay next to a bicycle.

At first, they saw only three people, and then they identified the source of the shrieks, a young girl pinned under the unmoving body of the woman. "Somebody call 911," yelled Greg as he moved swiftly to the woman's body and rolled it off the girl who continued screaming incoherently.

Her clothes were soaked in blood, and her bare arms were covered, which caused her to shriek even more when she saw it. Greg could find no injury, however, and lifted her off the ground and carried her away from the scene. The blood must have come from the woman who had covered her with her body. He sat her on the ground and tried to calm her. Eventually, she stopped screaming and began to cry, huge wracking sobs that shook her entire body.

The others still stood staring at the three bodies, fixated on the copious amounts of blood still spreading beneath them into the earth. A couple of the boys vomited in the trees and kept their backs turned. Jim pulled his cellphone out of his pocket and dialed 911.

Within ten minutes a police cruiser pulled into the parking lot beside the pond, and two policemen charged through the trees. An ambulance arrived a few moments later and finding no sign of life in the three adults, the EMS medics tended to the child who had lapsed into a state of shock.

CHAPTER 2

Krystal Murphy paused to stare up at the gleaming steel and glass façade of 300 South Tryon Street in the heart of Charlotte, North Carolina, before entering the marble clad lobby. She'd left her battered Volkswagen in the adjacent garage looking out of place in the company of the shiny, late model cars parked alongside.

She was ten minutes early for the first day of work at Private Security and Inquiries, the firm her friend, former CIA officer Robert Strachey, had established a few months earlier. She had solid and impressive credentials as a detective in the Arlington County Police Department where she'd risen from beat cop to Chief of Detectives investigating high-profile cases involving government corruption and even Russian espionage. So, why was she so nervous today?

Because, she thought, as she stood tapping her foot waiting for an elevator, she was making a complete break with her past, with a career she had so carefully cultivated and built, and entering a completely different world which held promise but still could be only dimly perceived, like a shapeless figure in the fog.

She'd splurged on a new pant suit before leaving Virginia, and she wore it now, feeling less confident than she looked. The elevator whisked her up to the 21st floor. The entrance to Private Security and Inquiries was directly opposite the elevator doors.

Krystal pushed through polished oak double doors into a lavishly furnished reception area that looked like a movie set. Strachey had carried a British men's club theme right to the front door. He had even paid to have a plank floor installed over the standard tile. She was used to a more utilitarian workplace, but Strachey was the boss, and it was his money, after all.

A mahogany trimmed reception desk sat in front of a green marble wall emblazoned with the firm's name in large, polished brass letters. At the desk was a woman who might be politely called "middle-aged" wearing a bright red suit. Her permed, gray hair was cut short to encircle a pleasant oval face with a pair of large, brown eyes that now peered at her through rhinestone encrusted glasses.

"Good mornin'," she said, "May I help you?"

"My name is Murphy. I think I'm expected."

The receptionist beamed at her, "Well," she said, giving the word an extra syllable, "we certainly have been expectin' you. I'm Ruth, by the way, Ruth Scatterfield. Let's get you right in to see Bob."

Without waiting she stood and headed for the set of double doors that evidently led to the offices. Krystal followed and after a short tour of the luxurious suite was soon seated in Robert Strachey's corner office where Ruth served them coffee at a polished, round table, and then left them alone.

The window behind Strachey offered a magnificent view of Charlotte. Strachey waved his arm and asked, "Well, what do you think?"

"Jesus, Bob," she said, "you must be making up for all those years in cramped government offices."

Strachey was amused. "There's probably some truth in that."

"Do your deep-pocketed clients know you worked for the CIA?"

"They know enough. It's good advertising in this business, and the more mysterious I make it, the more they like it."

"Do they know how you prevented a nuclear holocaust in Europe?"

Strachey frowned. Nobody outside of a small circle should ever know what he had done in Spain. "Dammit, my wife has been talking out of school," he said, "So, my answer is that I don't know what you're talking about, and we won't discuss it again, unless you want to lose your dental plan." The slash of a wide grin split his tanned face.

She raised her hands, palms out in surrender, and said, "OK, boss, whatever you say. My lips are sealed."

CHAPTER 3

"Want to see your new office?" Strachey asked, the grin still on his face.

"Sure."

He escorted her to the office next to his. "An office befitting my partner," he said.

Krystal was surprised. "Partner? I don't have any money to invest in this."

He shook his head dismissively. "I know, but you're a partner all the same. I think the term is 'salaried partner.' As such, I'll expect your unvarnished, honest to God opinion as an equal on things we're doing. And you will oversee investigations while I stick to the security stuff. We'll eventually hire some part-time investigators to work directly for you."

She was impressed by the level of confidence his gesture implied. She was feeling better about her decision.

"I'm expecting a client in a few minutes," he said. "I'll call you in once he's settled. You might as well get in the saddle right away."

He left, and she stood there in the middle of her office. The contrast with the Spartan office she had occupied at Arlington County Police Headquarters was stark. Out the window she could see beyond the outskirts of the city. The desk was made of some sort of dark wood rather than the gray metal government issue desk she was used to. There were shelves and a large, flat screen TV on the wall. She sat down in a mild state of shock recalling her last day in Arlington.

She stared at the cardboard box that sat squarely

in the middle of the desk. It had been provided by a thoughtful Arlington County Police Department for her to pack up any personal belongings she might have kept in her office. They could have spared the expense. The box was empty except for a ball point pen carrying the logo of a local bank and a pair of Domino's Pizza coupons. She didn't know whether to be amused or saddened by the pitiful display which might have suggested either that she was bereft of personality or personal life outside the office or preferred not to display it, indicating a secretive nature. She snorted and dumped the items from the box into the wastebasket.

Sergeant Frank Watson sat watching her, bonelessly sprawled on a chair as if his lanky, loose-limbed figure had been poured over it. Watson, a soft-spoken Georgia native fond of citing homely aphorisms, could make himself comfortable anywhere. He shot her a quizzical look out of the corner of his eye and drawled, "Is that it, Red? You got nothing else here?"

"Pitiful, isn't it," she said as she stared into the box. "This is it, the sum total of eight years, and this is all it amounts to."

"Did you have a farewell chat with the Chief?"

"Uh huh." Although she had expected nothing special, still it had been an anticlimactic moment.

The Chief had stood when she entered but didn't come out from behind his desk leading to an awkward handshake across its top. "I want to wish you good luck," he'd said with what looked suspiciously like a relieved smile. "You've had a good run here," he finished.

"Thanks, Chief." In fact, she had solved the most difficult and dangerous cases to confront the Department

in recent memory, more than once nearly losing her life. The problem was that she had raised her profile, and the public ate it up, which aroused envy. She'd exposed the murderous activities of the State's Attorney and her lover, the former Chief of Detectives. Not long thereafter, she had been promoted over the heads of others to the vacant position. It had not won many friends in the Department. A penchant for defying orders and proving herself right hadn't made any friends either.

The meeting with the Chief had lasted perhaps five minutes.

CHAPTER 4

After leaving the CIA, Robert Strachey joined his uncle's Washington lobbying firm and made a pile of money. But he missed the action of his old job and wanted to try something new. Now, after three months in Charlotte, he felt completely at home, as well he should as a North Carolina native, although his childhood had been spent in the mountains of the Piedmont rather than the gentility of Charlotte.

Strachey's uncle was a Charlotte luminary, and he'd lent a hand identifying some fat clients for his nephew's security and investigation firm. There were already three profitable contracts to provide security and background investigations for various companies.

Husbands in Charlotte still cheated on their wives and *vice versa*, people went missing, and insurance companies still wanted accident investigations before paying claims. Chasing down errant husbands was not as fulfilling as investigating homicides, and Strachey worried that Krystal would need bigger challenges.

This morning's visitor would certainly get his partner off on the right track. The name, of course, was familiar from recent newspaper headlines and television news reports. Murder attracted the public's attention.

There was a light knock at the door, and Ruth Scatterfield ushered a slight, dark man into the office. He was perhaps five feet eight inches tall, thin, with a narrow face dominated by large, dark, nearly black eyes under bushy brows. A shock of black hair streaked with gray fell across his forehead. He wore a suit of some dark, nearly black material. The visitor held himself upright and waited for Strachey to greet him.

"Mr. Nessmith," said Strachey, rising to shake his hand. "I've been expecting you. Please take a seat." He indicated the leather sofa that sat along one wall. Two comfortable leather chairs faced the sofa across an antique coffee table.

This was Padruig Nessmith. His appearance did not invite conviviality nor any suggestion that he sought friendship or needed it. Indeed, if those of dour countenance in the world wished for an avatar, Padruig Nessmith would have served them well. But today there was a reason for his long face, and Strachey knew exactly what it was.

Nessmith sat stiffly on the edge of the sofa, his body rigid and upright. Strachey took the chair opposite. "Would you care for a cup of coffee or tea?" he asked.

"No, thank you. I prefer to get straight to business. Your uncle suggested you might be able to help me. I assume you know why I'm here."

Nessmith's name had featured prominently in the press for the last week. Everybody loves a scandal, and by Charlotte's genteel standards, this was a big one. A week earlier while on a family picnic at one of the city's 'Greenway' parks, Nessmith's younger brother and his wife had been brutally murdered, and their young daughter traumatized. The longstanding feud between the Nessmith brothers, scions of a prominent Charlotte family, had long been a subject of gossip at the Charlotte Country Club and afternoon tea parties in Myers Park and Eastover.

"I think so," replied Strachey. "Would you mind

if I asked a colleague to sit in on this meeting?"

Nessmith shrugged and looked down at the floor.

Strachey called Ruth and told her to ask Krystal to join them. The ex-cop no longer favored her trademark jeans and polo shirt as she had in Arlington. He had been pleased to see her in a designer pant suit that flattered her figure and a creamy silk blouse. Her shoulder length auburn mane was stylishly coiffed, parted in the middle, and swept back from her forehead.

The men stood when she entered, and Strachey introduced her to Nessmith who reluctantly took her hand and shot a malevolent look at Strachey. "A woman? Why do we need her here?"

Obviously, Padruig Nessmith had little use for courtesy and maybe even less for women.

There was a slight but clear edge to Strachey's voice when he answered. "Miss Murphy is my trusted partner. She is a decorated former police detective lieutenant, and she will play a prominent role in your case, providing we agree to help you."

Nessmith grimaced and turned his attention to Krystal. His eyes did not stray over her body or linger on her breasts. Instead they bored into her as if he wanted to excavate her soul and examine it. With an effort, she did not avert her eyes and held his until he turned back to Strachey. "If you insist." He sat back down.

Strachey gestured for Krystal to take the chair beside his across from Nessmith. "Krystal," he said, "we were about to discuss the reason for Mr. Nessmith's visit." To Nessmith, "Please go, on."

The strange man's words were uttered in a low monotone without a trace of emotion. "As you undoubtedly know from the press, my younger brother and his wife were murdered last weekend. The ill feeling that has existed for years between my brother and myself is well known, as is the fact that I wanted to buy his half of the business, which he refused to consider. With his death, his shares come to me. Unfortunately, it seems this somehow makes me the prime suspect in the crime, both in the minds of the police and the eyes of the public, thanks to disgraceful and baseless media speculation. I may be arrested at any moment, and my attorney says there is nothing to be done to prevent it."

"You don't have an alibi for the time of the murders?" asked Strachey.

Krystal maintained an unaccustomed silence. Padruig Nessmith was the most unattractive and disagreeable man she had ever encountered, a fact which could not help but engender prejudice against him. He made the perfect villain. The dark little man raised her hackles, and she hoped Strachey did not take the case.

"I was at home alone," replied Nessmith with a trace of defiance. "I seldom leave the house on weekends."

Nothing in the man's demeanor or words encouraged the idea that he might be innocent. There was not a trace to be seen of sorrow about the murder of his younger brother and his wife, nor concern for the fate of their daughter.

"Thank you, Mr. Nessmith," said Strachey. "Give us a day or so to review your case. We'll be wanting a more in-depth interview with you, by the way. We'll need elaboration on some details. So, if you don't mind, we'll stop by your house in the morning."

"Why do you need to interview me?" asked Nessmith. "I don't like the idea. What I want you to do is find the real killer so everybody will leave me alone."

"Mr. Nessmith, if we are to help you, we must know everything and anything that might impinge on the case. If we are to prove your innocence, we need to know who you are and all the circumstances of your relationship with your brother."

This was something Nessmith obviously found distasteful. For an instant Krystal thought/hoped he would refuse, and that would be the end of it. But after a moment's hesitation, he relented. "All right," he muttered, "I'll expect you at ten in the morning." He stood and walked out of the office without another word.

When he was gone Krystal said, "You're not going to take his case, are you? What a weird bird."

"It could be interesting, Krystal, and worthwhile. The Nessmiths can afford to pay a lot."

"We don't have any financial problems, do we? We can't be that desperate."

"We're running a business here, and we can't afford to turn away clients. And there's something else. This is a big case. It's all over the news. If we can squeeze a success out of it, it will mean good publicity for the firm."

"And if we can't, it'll mean the opposite."

"Well, it's going to be up to you."

"What?"

"This is going to be your case. You like a challenge, and I think the Nessmith matter has Krystal Murphy written all over it. You'll have fun."

"Fun? Working with that little creep?"

"I want you to interview him tomorrow, and then

we'll try to find a useful contact in the police. Now, go to your office and read everything you can find on the murders. The press is calling them 'the picnic murders.' After you've finished interviewing Padruig, I want you to go talk to my aunt Sadie. There's nothing about people in Charlotte and the gossip about them she doesn't know, and I'm sure old Padruig is a hot topic these days. You might find out something interesting. In the meantime, I'll set something up with the police.

CHAPTER 5

Padruig Nessmith lived with his sister, Gavenia, in one of the older houses in Myers Park. It was smaller than its newer neighbors but retained an air of faded gentility with its large portico supported by four round white columns. The house was of wooden construction, which lent it even more of an antique air.

Krystal rang the bell, and the door was opened by a thin, dark woman of around sixty wearing a severe black dress. Given the physical resemblance to Padruig, Krystal assumed this was Gavenia, but the woman did not introduce herself. After confirming Krystal's identity, she wordlessly led the way to a large living room just off the entrance foyer. None of the furnishings looked less than a hundred years old. The curtains were drawn blocking the morning's bright sunlight in favor of gloom.

Padruig stood in the middle of the room looking as malevolent as ever. Krystal imagined him hanging from the ceiling like a bat. He greeted her entry with a curt nod before inviting her to sit on a settee covered in patterned silk. "I hope this won't take long," he said without a trace of apology. "I have business to attend to."

"You asked us to help you, Mr. Nessmith. That's what we're trying to do and why I'm here, but you're going to have to cooperate." If he could be obstinate, so could she.

"Cooperate! It's foolish," he growled. "I've done nothing wrong. I had nothing to do with the murder of my brother and that woman. The only reason I went to you is because my attorney said I should find someone, and Lyle Strachey recommended his nephew."

Why did he refer to his sister-in-law as 'that woman?' "You obviously heeded your lawyer's advice. So, why don't you sit down and answer some questions?"

"Oh, very well. But it won't change anything." He perched on the edge of an upholstered chair, reminding her of a crow on a power line.

"You told us you were here in the house all weekend but that no one saw you. Where was your sister? You do share this house."

"Gavenia spent the weekend at our house in Asheville. She has, er, friends there."

And she was probably glad to get away from you. The thought sprang up unbidden.

"Did you go outside? Is it possible a neighbor saw you here?"

"Young lady, this house sits in the middle of a wooded acre of land and is well-screened, thank God, from neighborhood prying. Regardless, I did not leave the house."

"Did you receive any phone calls, or was there a delivery of some sort during that time?"

"No."

"Mr. Nessmith, can you think of anything, anything at all that might confirm your alibi? Did you make any phone calls, for example?"

"No."

As the desultory interview continued Krystal fought to control her temper. What sort of creature was this Padruig Nessmith? He was the strangest character she had ever met, and that included a lot of very strange individuals, including Iranian assassins, Russian spies, and crazy CIA guys. The man seemed not to belong to this world nor wish to. What had happened to him to cause him to retreat from the human race? Was he capable of murder? She had no clue. Her gut was usually reliable and although Nessmith was unlikeable, he also gave off no vibes. It was like trying to relate to a tree stump.

*****

When the inquisitive woman left, Padruig Nessmith did not move. He stood in the center of the darkened room with his head bowed in thought. The situation was intolerable. It was intolerable that the police and press should invade his privacy and matters that should remain within the family, what was left of it. He was still uncertain of the wisdom of hiring a private detective, even though his attorney had strongly recommended it. There could be no evidence that he had committed a crime, and he was determined to provide no information that might point to the contrary. It was impossible that he could be arrested and dragged before the public, everything exposed. It was a long time since he had felt vulnerable, a long time, and he had vowed never to permit it again.

He didn't notice when Gavenia entered the room and was startled when she spoke. "You should tell them," she said.

Was there a tinge of fear or apprehension in her voice? Could she be trusted to follow his course.

He turned to face her. "There is no need. It would only complicate things."

"But you were not here all weekend." Gavenia

wrung her hands and a crease appeared between her eyes. "You drove to Asheville to pick me up."

"No one saw me but you, sister," he said. "It would be foolish to admit I was out of the house when the murders took place. It would only complicate the situation." He turned toward her, and his hard stare made her feel like a butterfly pinned to a sheet of paper.

She returned his stare uncertainly, and Padruig read doubt in her eyes. He softened his tone. "Don't worry, sister. Everything will be all right. Nothing will happen."

After she left the room Nessmith sank heavily into a chair and leaned his head back and closed his eyes. But his mind conjured up that horrible scene in the church so many years ago, and it caused him almost physical pain. It would all be dredged up again, he knew, and his humiliation would be revisited. Alive or dead, his brother and sister-in-law brought him nothing but anguish.

*****

Next stop was Strachey's aunt Sadie, and Krystal did not have to travel far. Lyle and Sadie Strachey also lived in Myers Park, one of the moneyed enclaves of Charlotte and perhaps the most traditional one. The tree-lined boulevard was lined with multi-million-dollar mansions on large lots. Strachey's uncle Lyle and his wife occupied a white stone home of gargantuan proportions. Krystal often wondered how people could possibly require so much space. To someone who had grown up on a farm in southern Indiana where every inch had a purpose, the fact that Lyle and Sadie

Strachey who had no children made their home in a five-bedroom behemoth was nearly incomprehensible and roused in her a slight contempt rather than envy.

Sadie Strachey opened the door and greeted Krystal with a bright smile. She was petite, and at somewhere over sixty, still vivacious. She wore a white sleeveless dress and a pink scarf around her neck. "Bobby said you would be stopping by. Come on in. I have coffee and sweet rolls waiting." Her accent was syrupy sweet. It took Krystal a moment to realize that 'Bobby' was Robert Strachey. She had vaguely prepared herself to dislike Strachey's aunt, but the warm greeting and the woman's bubbly demeanor immediately disarmed her.

Sadie led her through the house to a flag-stoned patio in the back that overlooked a manicured half acre which boasted two large magnolia trees, an abundance of flowering azaleas, and a kidney-shaped swimming pool. A silver coffee service and a plate of sweets awaited them on a table beneath a colorful umbrella. Sadie carefully poured the coffee into porcelain cups and used tongs to set a strawberry tart on Krystal's plate. "If it were afternoon," said Sadie with a twinkle in her eye, "we would be having mai-tais or sangria." She waved Krystal to one of the cushioned chairs around the table. "Now that we're all comfy, Bobby said you wanted to talk about Padruig Nessmith. Is that right?"

"Yes," nodded Krystal. "Anything you can tell me about him would be useful."

"Well, dear, there's this awful murder thing, and everyone is certain he must have done it. Poor Padruig doesn't have many admirers."

"So I gathered. He's not a very likable person, is he? Why do you say 'poor Padruig'?"

Sadie took a dainty bite of her pastry and sipped her coffee before answering. "What do you know about his family?"

"I'm new to Charlotte, but I gather he is quite wealthy."

"That's true. His father immigrated from Scotland in the fifties and opened a little hardware shop here in town. Charlotte was a much smaller and quieter place in those days. Some of our folks were pioneers and trailblazers in the banking sector for the entire Piedmont, and by the seventies things really started to happen. By the end of the nineties Charlotte was headquarters to the first nationwide bank, the Bank of America, and we just continued to grow. Padruig's father, also named Padruig, grew with the city's prosperity. He was a wily old coot and soon branched out with a string of hardware stores in town and kept growing until he controlled a retail empire throughout the state and down into South Carolina. He made a fortune. His three children, Padruig, Gavenia, and the youngest brother, Jaidon led privileged lives. Padruig was the eldest sibling and was soon helping his father run the business. In those days he was considered quite a catch by the young ladies. He was a good athlete and had the kind of dark good looks women go for. He was quite popular. I remember him well from those days."

Krystal nearly choked on her coffee. "Padruig Nessmith was popular and sought after by women? What the ... what happened? He's one of the least attractive men I've ever met."

Sadie shook her head sadly and clicked her tongue. "And that's a tragedy. It's an old, old story, my dear. As usual, there was a woman involved. Her name was Tennant, Christanna Tennant, and she was an empty-headed southern belle but very beautiful. Padruig fell madly in love with her despite the huge difference in their ages and proposed marriage, which she accepted. But she jilted him in the worst possible way. She left Padruig standing at the altar and ran away with his much younger brother, Jaidon, who was almost as empty-headed as she. They made a fine pair." Sadness mingled with indignation colored her words. "Padruig was never the same afterwards. It was as though his soul had curdled and could never be restored. He disappeared from society and spent all his energies on the business, seldom appearing in public. At first, his old friends were sorry for him, but he could not be drawn out, and eventually they lost interest. In the end, he became an object of ridicule, poor thing. Of course, the brothers became estranged. I doubt they have spoken to one another since.

"But when their father died, he bequeathed the business to both boys, giving them equal shares. There were two conditions to the will: first, the boys were to take care of their sister, Gavenia, ensuring that she would never want for anything. Old man Nessmith didn't believe in permitting women in business, but he did care for his daughter, and poor Gavenia never married. The other condition was that the business could never be sold or broken up unless Padruig and Jaidon agreed. Of course, Padruig continued to run the business and Jaidon, who had never shown an interest, lived off the dividends. Their father obviously hoped the boys eventually would reconcile."

Nessmith's reference to his deceased sister-in-law as 'that woman' was explained, and Krystal wondered how deeply the vein of hatred ran in Padruig Nessmith. "Do you think he killed his brother?" asked Krystal.

"It's been such a long time ... I wouldn't blame him. Would you?" Sadie cocked her head and shot her a questioning look under an arched and well plucked eyebrow.

"He definitely had motive, didn't he?"

"Well," said Sadie with a tight smile. "Don't you think that if he had murderous intent against Jaidon he would have done something immediately rather than waiting for over twenty years?"

"Not necessarily," replied Krystal. "Hatred can grow and fester over time until it overpowers a person's better instincts. Grudges, especially those that rise out of a deep wound, only become bigger."

Sadie sighed, "Yes, I suppose you're right. What Jaidon and Christanna did to him was unforgivable. It certainly wounded him and changed him completely. I've always suspected that the young Padruig had a gentle, trusting nature. When betrayed such people have a hard time recovering, and I think Padruig's heart must have been broken right in two."

"Thank you, Mrs. Strachey. You've been very helpful. It makes it a little easier to understand Padruig." Krystal was surprised to find herself for the first time feeling some sympathy for their strange, uncommunicative client. But the undeniable takeaway was that she had discovered a strong motive for murder. There was a lot to think about.

CHAPTER 6

Strachey had arranged a meeting early in the afternoon at Charlotte Mecklenburg Police headquarters on East Trade Street. Krystal joined him for lunch at Fitzgerald's, a place on East 5th that despite pretensions to be an Irish bar lacked the cozy intimacy of the real thing. But there was Guinness on tap and the food was acceptable. Strachey ordered a beer and burger while Krystal had a Cobb salad and a coke. She was trying to cut down on alcohol, especially Scotch. Avoiding beer was at least a start.

Through a mouthful of burger Strachey asked, "So, what did you find out?"

"Our client is a character, a very unlikable and uncooperative character who bears a striking resemblance to Ebenezer Scrooge. And according to your aunt he had strong motives to murder his brother, both personal and financial." She went on to relate the tale of Padruig Nessmith's betrayal at the altar.

The Charlotte Mecklenburg Police are headquartered in an unimaginative but utilitarian, white concrete building across the street from a small green park in a pristine section of the city called Government Plaza crowded with modern buildings with a lot of straight lines and angles. They left the car in a parking lot at the rear and walked around to the columned main entrance. She'd never been there before, but as soon as they entered the building she was in familiar territory. The utilitarian interior with its uniformed occupants felt and smelled like home. Not for the first time she wondered if she'd made the right decision to leave Arlington. She still felt like a cop. It was all she had known her entire adult life.

An officer directed them to the Homicide/ADW Unit where they found Captain Abel Curry waiting to greet them. Curry was a big man of considerable bulk with a shiny, shaved pate and dark five o'clock shadow. He was probably in his mid-fifties, but the shaved head made it difficult to judge. "Come on into my office," he said, his tone formal, and gestured them through a door with frosted glass panels and the Captain's name in neat, black letters. The faint aroma of tobacco greeted them, and Krystal noticed an open window suggesting that Captain Curry regularly abused the no smoking rule. This inclined her positively toward the man. There was a large, wooden desk with neatly stacked papers, a flat-screen television mounted on the wall opposite the desk, and a scarred wooden conference table that bore a multitude of rings from coffee cups and glasses, as well as cigarette burns across its surface. Incongruously, a large vase with a flower arrangement occupied its center. They were begonias, and Krystal suspected they were from Curry's garden. The floor was covered in green, industrial grade carpeting.

A uniformed cop with sergeant's stripes rose from the couch and raked them with policeman's eyes set deeply in a narrow face. In contrast to Curry, he was bone thin with closely cropped blond hair. "This is Sergeant Archie Wolf, my Chief of Staff," said Curry with a careless wave in the man's direction.

Strachey introduced them and, the amenities observed, they took seats around the table.

"Thank you for agreeing to meet with us, Captain Curry," began Strachey. "We're grateful for the time.

The reason we're here is ..."

"I know why you're here," interrupted Curry. "It's the so-called picnic murders, and you've been hired by Padruig Nessmith."

"That's right," nodded Strachey.

Curry continued as though Strachey had not spoken. "Frankly, I don't see there is much you can do that isn't already being done. We have an experienced and capable homicide unit here, and we're leaving no stone unturned in this case. As a matter of fact, I'm heading up the investigation myself and have formed a task force of a half-dozen of my best detectives under the supervision of Sergeant Wolf here."

Krystal instinctively liked Curry. Strachey was good, but he didn't know cops like she did. "We understand," she said with a glance at Strachey that said, *'let me handle this.'* "I was a cop, the head of a homicide unit, and I know where you're coming from. We have no intention of stepping on any toes or interfering with your investigation. All we ask is that you share with us whatever you reasonably can about the case. All we know is what's in the news, but you can't trust those bozos." She was counting on cops' universally shared antipathy toward the press. "Our client insists he had nothing to do with the murders. If we find anything to the contrary, we'll share it with you. We want to stay well in the background."

Curry could not suppress a slight grin at her opinion of the press, and Wolf raised his eyebrows when she said she had been a cop.

"You were a cop? Whereabouts?" asked Curry.

"Arlington County Police just outside of Washington." She had no doubt that Curry would check her *bona fides*.

"The only reason I agreed to this meeting was because the Chief ordered it," said Curry with a squinty-eyed glance at Strachey. "Mr. Strachey's uncle carries a lot of weight in this town, and he golfs with the Chief. I can give you the basic information, but I won't be sharing any confidential details of our investigation."

"Understood," nodded Strachey. The reference to his uncle Lyle grated on him. "So, why don't you tell us everything you can, and we'll get out of your way?"

A long, audible sigh escaped from Curry. Sergeant Wolf had yet to utter a word as he studied them with Arctic blue eyes. "You know we're looking into three murders. As best we can piece it together, based on the scene, Jaidon and Christanna Nessmith were enjoying a picnic lunch with their daughter when they were accosted and shot point blank in the head. It appears that they had no chance to escape their killer. The third victim was riding his bicycle through the Greenway when he came upon the scene, and the killer went after him. He had two wounds, one in the back, and another through the head, poor bastard. He was in the wrong place at the wrong time."

"Any witnesses?" asked Krystal. "The daughter survived. Did she see anything?"

"The child is only eleven years old. Apparently, when the shooting started, her mother threw herself on top of her. The poor kid lay there under her dead mother until she was rescued. She can't tell us anything, and she's in shock, still under a doctor's care. There was a pick-up softball game at one of the fields there, but they were a long way away. The park is big, over 120 acres. They heard the shots, but by the time anyone got to the scene the perp had disappeared."

"That's terrible. What about the weapon?" asked Krystal

"Forensics say it was probably a .38 Special," replied Curry.

"Did the killer take anything? The Nessmiths were wealthy."

"Nothing," replied Curry. "It could have been a robbery gone wrong, and the killer didn't have time to take anything, of course. He had to get out of there before anyone showed up. He must have known someone would hear the shots."

"Strange. Why didn't he just hold the Nessmiths at gunpoint and rob them? Why fire the gun and attract attention?"

"And that suggests," smiled Curry, "that there may have been a motive other than robbery."

"What's known about the third victim, the bike rider?" asked Krystal.

"Not much there. Name was Gregory Davis, an accountant at H.P.S National Bank downtown, married, no known enemies. Bike riding enthusiast. He'd only moved to Charlotte a little over a year ago. Other than that, there's not much to know."

*****

They drove south from police headquarters to the scene of the murders, one of Charlotte's many 'greenways,' swaths of natural woodlands and water preserved for public recreation. Strachey asked, "Any thoughts?"

She wrinkled her brow. "Nothing worth saying

out loud. You know the old 48-hour rule about solving a murder. We're beyond that now, and every day that passes puts it farther from a resolution. I have a feeling nothing about this is going to be easy. It's just weird."

"What do you think about what Curry said - the Nessmiths were shot at close range, once to the head each, but the guy on the bike was hit twice?

"He was probably trying to get away like Curry said."

He nodded, concentrating on his driving. "If I had to guess, I'd say the police have nothing more to go on than we at this point."

It was another warm, cloudless day which made for a pleasant drive along Park Road to the scene of the crime, just south of Tyvolia Road. They pulled onto the access drive and parked in a large tarmacked area next to a pond. There were only two other cars in the lot, and the park looked otherwise deserted.

"It's a week-day," said Krystal. "Just like the day of the killings."

"Yeah, hardly anyone here. Must have been the same then."

They spent a half-hour strolling around the park. There were basketball courts, baseball fields, playgrounds and picnic shelters. There was another parking lot on the other side of the pond, and yet another near the baseball fields. There were still shreds of yellow crime scene tape on the east bank of the pond, not far from the lot where they left their car.

"This isn't far from the exit," noted Strachey. "The killer could have been in his car and out of the park in a few minutes."

Jaidon and Christanna Nessmith had chosen a

shaded spot beside the water for their picnic. "Lots of cover," said Krystal pointing at the trees and shrubbery between the parking lot and the path around the pond. The shooter could have walked from the parking lot through the trees without the victims ever seeing him. He took them completely by surprise."

"And the bike rider had the misfortune of coming along the path at the time of the shooting."

"Looks that way, yeah."

They studied the site, Krystal searching instinctively for clues, spent shell casings, anything. But there was nothing. "Curry's guys went over the site well," she said. "He said they found no shell casings, so the weapon was most likely a revolver like he said. I don't think the shooter would have stayed around picking up brass."

"He must be a damn good shot," said Strachey. "One shot each for the Nessmiths and two for the bike rider who must have tried to escape."

"Yeah, well, it's pretty close range. The shooter would only have to be reasonably skillful."

Strachey chewed this over. "Maybe. The bastard made a clean getaway. Do you think it would be useful to interview the softball team?"

"The ones who were practicing here? I dunno. Curry said they saw nothing."

"They heard the shots. Maybe that would tell us something."

"It was a .38 special according to Curry. Pretty common gun."

He frowned. "Damn little to go on. Best thing is to start interviewing people who knew the victims."

"We'll just be repeating what Curry's

investigators are doing. You know, this still could have been just a mugging gone wrong by some thug who didn't even know his victims."

Krystal scanned the area again considering the possibilities. "Maybe, but when you consider the location, the setting, the short distance to the parking lot and the cover, we might be looking at a well-planned ambush."

"So, premeditated murder," said Strachey in a low tone. "It's certainly a possibility when you look at it that way. And that means someone who knew the victims, someone with a motive strong enough to justify murder."

"Curry's guys would not have missed the possibility," said Krystal. "You can bet they're knocking on doors."

"With the Nessmith family involved, you can bet those are high society doors."

"And so far, the only person we know of who had a strong motive is Padruig, and the story your aunt told me must be very well known among Charlotte's old families."

"Without a doubt."

CHAPTER 7

It was late afternoon and a light summer rain splattered against the office windows making little shushing sounds before trickling in squiggly ranks down the glass. Krystal had spent another fruitless morning interviewing people who obviously could have no direct knowledge of the murders of Jaidon and Christanna Nessmith but nevertheless felt obliged to share their conviction that it only could have been Padruig whose years of silent simmering rage finally had boiled over with deadly consequences in the best traditions of the Southern Gothic novel. The murders and press speculation had rejuvenated the tale of Christanna abandoning Padruig at the altar to run away with his younger brother and bolstered the idea of a modern Cain and Abel story right here in Billy Graham's hometown.

She was preparing to write a report that would provide exactly zero useful information when the phone rang. It was Abel Curry calling from his office at police HQS. "Hello, Miss Murphy, I thought I should give you a heads up."

Her immediate thought was that there had been a break in the case, and she was not mistaken. "We're bringing Padruig Nessmith in as we speak. Suspicion of murder."

There was evident satisfaction in his voice.

She sat up straight. The police had held off until now because of lack of evidence. Suspicion alone was enough to justify further investigation but not an arrest. Something had changed. "What have you found out?"

she asked.

Curry didn't answer immediately. "I can't say over the phone, but if you want to come over here, I'll fill you in as a courtesy to a former cop."

Strachey was out with a client and she didn't want to disturb him. Best if she had some real information to report before talking to him. "OK, Captain, I'm on my way. And thanks."

"No problem."

A bond of sorts, a cops' bond, existed between her and the shiny-pated Abel Curry. She knew how the game was played, and the Captain appreciated the fact. She and Strachey had been careful not to step on official toes and to keep Curry abreast of what they were doing. It was paying off.

Curry was waiting for her with a fresh pot of coffee and a plate of donuts. They sat at his conference table, and the Captain got straight to business. "I'm doing this as a courtesy to you and Strachey," he began, "but the information is confidential, and I want you to promise not to share it with anyone but Strachey."

"Sure," she said. "I promise."

He inspected her with a pro's eyes and apparently was satisfied with what he saw. "I never believed Padruig's claim that he was home alone on the day of the murders. So, I assigned a man to check traffic cam footage. We have quite a few cameras around the city covering the main intersections and heavy traffic areas. It took a few days, but he finally spotted Padruig in his car heading out of town just after the murders took place." His lips shaped themselves into a grim smile. "They should be booking him about now."

The information was unwelcome, but not unexpected. Krystal had doubted Padruig was telling the truth, too, and the man's uncooperative attitude reinforced the impression. He didn't even seem to be trying ... or he just did not care.

"Do you think he'll get bail?"

Curry selected a frosted cruller from the plate, chewed for a few seconds, followed it with a swig of black coffee and then shook his head. "I don't know. Depends on the judge. There won't be an arraignment until tomorrow morning, so he'll spend at least the night in a cell."

"Have you ever met him? Talked to him?"

"Nope."

"Don't expect much."

"I understand he's a truculent sort."

"You got that right."

"So," he asked around another mouthful of cruller, "what will you and Strachey do now?"

She frowned. "Dunno. I gotta talk with him about it."

"Think you'll drop your client?"

Good question. "That'll be up to Strachey. We'll let you know. Is it possible to talk to Padruig?"

"That's a question for his lawyer. You'll have to talk to him."

She drove slowly back to the office wondering if it was quite right for her to be neither surprised nor concerned about Padruig Nessmith's arrest. She'd found no common ground nor the slightest possibility of empathy with him. Other people got over heartbreak without shutting themselves off from the world. Other people permitted their friends to sympathize and help.

But Padruig Nessmith had allowed himself to become an unlikable little troglodyte whose emotions were as fenced in as North Korea. He distrusted everything and everyone even, as Curry's new evidence showed, to the point of not sharing the truth with people trying to help him. But now he would need all the help she and Strachey could give him, providing he was indeed innocent, and she was having some doubts about that. He had lied not only to them, but also to the police, and that lie was enough to provoke his arrest. She could not help but speculate about why he had lied. Curry had said Nessmith had been seen on the street shortly after the killings. It was only a few minutes' drive from the murder scene to the intersection where he had been caught on the traffic camera according to Curry. She had no idea how Strachey would receive the news. There were still some things to straighten out before she would be satisfied that she had left no stone unturned.

She didn't have long to wait before Strachey returned to the office. He was whistling a little tune until he saw her. "Uh-oh," he said, "Something's up, and from the look on your face it isn't good. Spill it."

"Padruig's been arrested. He's been booked and is sitting in the county lock-up by now."

"They arrested him? On what evidence?"

She told him about the traffic camera.

"Damn!" He sat behind his desk and rummaged in a drawer for a box of cigars. She sat silently as he went through the ritual of lighting up. "Why in hell didn't he tell us he'd been out of the house?" he said. "What an idiot. He's treating us as if we were enemies."

"I don't think he trusts anyone, with the possible

exception of his sister."

"You think you should have a chat with her?"

Krystal chewed the inside of her cheek. "I suppose it wouldn't hurt. She hardly said a word when I was at the house."

"Can we see Padruig, maybe get some more information out of him now he's in jail?"

"Curry said we would have to go through his lawyer, and not until after the arraignment tomorrow morning in any case."

"Maybe they'll let him out on bail."

"I dunno. It's a high-profile case. I can't wait to see the papers tomorrow morning."

"They'll skewer the old boy, that's for sure."

"And the news will be received with glee by certain segments of Charlotte's upper crust. They've already convicted him in their minds."

Strachey took a few unenthusiastic puffs on his cigar and then laid it in the marble ashtray on his desk where it went cold and died. "I think we both should be at the courthouse tomorrow morning, and then, with some luck, we can see him."

*****

The Mecklenburg County Courthouse is conveniently located a stone's throw from the jail in another of those triangular Lego block buildings that give Charlotte's Government Plaza its character or lack thereof. At ten o'clock in the morning Padruig Nessmith was arraigned before the Honorable Elizabeth Cartwright in a small courtroom on the third floor. It was still drizzling rain when Krystal and Strachey parked and walked inside to find seats just behind the defendant's table. Most of the other seats were occupied by media representatives. Gavenia sat in a back row twisting a handkerchief between her fingers.

Padruig's attorney, Matthew Holmes, was already there looking somber in a navy-blue suit, crisp white shirt and red striped tie. They had met Holmes only once when they first took the case, and the man had seemed grateful they were on the team. Krystal found his soft North Carolina drawl disarming. He had explained that Padruig was as stubbornly close-mouthed with him as he was with them, something he attributed to pride. He was unhappy with his client, but his firm had been associated with the Nessmiths for decades, and this was a burden he was obliged to take on. He had called Strachey the evening before to ask them to attend the arraignment.

Holmes stood to greet them. Shaking his head of carefully coiffed silver hair as he extended his hand to Strachey, he said, "I'm glad to see you here. Thanks for coming."

"We would have come anyway," replied Strachey. "Do you have any more information?"

Holmes looked grave. "I'm afraid not. I'm sure you know as much as I do. I can't understand why Padruig wasn't straight with us. We could have taken steps to mitigate all this, but he lied, and that damages his case. It makes it look like he had something to hide. Has your investigation turned up anything helpful?"

Krystal shrugged. "He's too unsympathetic to have friends, if he ever had any at all. Most of the people we've interviewed have already made up their minds that he's guilty, and the media aren't helping things."

Holmes's shoulders slumped. "Yeah, that sounds about right. I would have been surprised if you had found anything. I'm not convinced he can be convicted solely on the evidence of a traffic camera photograph, but it will be rough sailing, nevertheless. He's the only suspect the police have. But if he didn't do it, someone else surely did. If you could discover another suspect, it would take some pressure off Padruig."

"That would be the ideal," agreed Strachey. "If Padruig wants us to continue, we can expand the investigation."

"I spoke with him earlier today," said Holmes. "He wants you to continue. He won't admit it, but he's worried as hell."

At that moment the Judge entered the chambers and the bailiff announced her. When she was seated, Padruig's case was called.

Two bailiffs emerged from a side door with a manacled Padruig Nessmith between them. He was wearing an orange prison jumpsuit that was clearly a size or two too large and made his thin figure seem even smaller. His face was inscrutable though his lips were white with what might have been repressed anger. His dark eyes swept over Krystal and Strachey before he turned and sat next to Holmes.

The arraignment was swift. The judge took Holmes's plea for bail under advisement, but Padruig would have to spend at least another night in jail. The judge also ordered a psychological evaluation which caused the color to rise on Padruig's neck.

CHAPTER 8

Krystal found Gregory Davis's house in a mixed neighborhood of older homes with neat lawns and lots of trees and decorative foliage. The Davis house was a single-story brick trimmed clapboard with a carport on one side under which was parked a white Honda Civic with a bicycle rack mounted on the rear. Two bikes hung from hooks in the carport ceiling. Krystal was a veteran at interviewing bereaved families, but it never got any easier. In this case, at least, she was not the notifying officer. She parked in the macadam driveway under the branches of a large oak tree and stepped out of the car. There was a sidewalk leading from the driveway to a brick semi-circular cement pad under an awning with three steps leading up to the front door. The space between the walk and the house was filled with azaleas and roses that blazed colorfully in the bright sunlight.

Her knock was answered by a slim woman in her early to mid-30's with long, dark hair, a pale complexion, and startling green eyes. She opened the glass-paneled door and looked inquiringly at Krystal. "Yes?"

"My name is Krystal Murphy." She handed the woman her card. "Are you Mrs. Gregory Davis?"

The woman studied the card, reading it carefully as though she did not understand the words. "You are detective?"

The accent was heavy and certainly derived from somewhere well beyond the Elbe. "Yes," said Krystal. "My company has been hired to investigate the

Michael R. Davidson

circumstances of the deaths of your husband and the other victims."

Mrs. Davis chewed on the information for a moment before asking, "You work with police?"

"We are cooperating with the police, but we are not affiliated with them. We're a private investigative service. May I come inside so we can talk?"

The woman didn't budge but returned her attention to the card, silently sounding out the words with her lips. "Why are you investigating this?"

"We've been hired by a member of the other victims' family." Krystal did not like dissimulating with the wife of a victim, but Mrs. Davis's hesitation worried her, and, after all Padruig Nessmith was a member of the victims' family. "It's very important, Mrs. Davis, that I speak with you."

Mrs. Davis raised uncertain eyes to Krystal. "I am not sure," she said. "I cannot right now. Is not good time." She stepped back inside and closed the door, leaving a surprised Krystal staring at her own reflection in the glass. She raised her hand to knock again but changed her mind. The woman did not want to talk.

*****

"We really need to talk to her. I just don't understand her attitude." Krystal failed to keep the frustration out of her voice.

She'd gone straight back to the office following her fruitless visit to Gregory Davis's wife and sat facing Strachey across his desk. Floor to ceiling cherry wood bookshelves lined two walls and two soft leather-covered wing chairs sat in the corner facing one another over an antique table with a brass reading lamp. Across the room with the window behind it stood the ornate mahogany desk. A crimson oriental rug glowed in the light streaming through the windows. A vase of fresh cut flowers sat in the middle of the table, colorful in the afternoon sunlight.

Strachey lit a short cigar as Krystal related her experience.

"You say she speaks with an accent?" he asked.

"Yes. She sounded like one of those Russians in the movies."

Strachey took a drag on the cigar and exhaled blue smoke that drifted in shifting layers in the beams of light before being sucked into the ventilators in the ceiling. "Hmmm. Could be a Russian mail-order bride, I suppose. Funny that Captain Curry didn't mention it. What's her name?"

"Natalie, Natalie Davis."

"Natalie, Natalya, Natasha. Interesting. Russians have a healthy distrust of the authorities, especially the police. I suppose that could explain her reluctance."

"I don't know. She was more wary than she was hostile, like talking to me was something she wasn't supposed to do."

"Curious. We'll need to get back to her. Maybe Curry will help smooth the way. In the meantime, we need to talk with Davis's fellow workers at the bank."

*****

The H.P.H. National Bank had its own skyscraper on South Tryon Street in the center of

Charlotte. Krystal entered the cavern-like lobby, all polished black marble and brass fittings. She'd been in Charlotte long enough not to be overwhelmed by the sheer size of the place or the ostentatious gold-toned chandeliers suspended from the twenty-foot ceiling. The bank intended the lobby to impress, and it usually did the job. There was a rank of turnstiles across the far end guarding the elevators and a reception counter manned by four people along one wall. Krystal approached the counter and identified herself. "I have an appointment with Mr. Stevens." She'd called earlier in the day to request a meeting with Davis's supervisor and been directed to Kim Stevens, who had identified himself as the head of the Internal Audit Division.

The honey blonde behind the counter flashed a set of brilliant white teeth that probably paid for her dentist's vacation to the Bahamas and asked for her identification. "A driver's license will be fine," she said.

With the formalities completed, the blonde handed her a plastic badge marked "Visitor" in bright red letters against a white field. There was a magnetic strip along one side of the card.

"Just run the card through the scanner at the turnstile," instructed the blonde. "Then take the elevator to the third floor."

It turned out that the elevator from the lobby only went to the third floor, and when she stepped out, she found herself in what she later learned was the "security lobby." Krystal reflected that it was harder to get into this bank than into FBI Headquarters in Washington. She again identified herself, this time to a serious young man behind a counter and was instructed to take a seat because there would be a short wait.

Along one wall facing the floor-to-ceiling windows overlooking Tryon Street was a suite of chrome framed couches and chairs upholstered in black leather and low, glass-topped tables displaying a variety of surprisingly up-to-date magazines. Krystal groaned inwardly, hoping this did not augur a long wait.

She was not disappointed. Within a few moments a man in a navy-blue suit, white shirt, and colorful Hermes tie emerged from the elevators behind yet another row of turnstiles. He consulted briefly with the man behind the counter, who pointed at Krystal. The man strode toward her, hand outstretched. "I'm Kim Stevens. Won't you come with me?"

She guessed Stevens' age at somewhere between forty and forty-five. His six-foot frame was well-proportioned, and he sported a tan most likely acquired on the golf course.

He led her back to the counter where she exchanged the plastic visitor's badge from the lobby for another plastic card marked "Escort Required," and Stevens directed her to the turnstile. Stevens wore his security card around his neck on a narrow chain lanyard. They each swiped their cards and went through the turnstile to the elevators. Inside, Stevens punched a button for the 12th floor, and they glided silently upward.

They emerged into a large open space occupied by cubicles with about fifty people milling about among them. Stevens led her to an office in the far corner and invited her to sit in yet another chrome and black leather chair. The office was utilitarian but upscale with a magnificent view of north Charlotte out the window.

Stevens introduced himself as the head of the Internal Audit Group which in turn was under Risk Management in the bank's hierarchy. "I understand you want to talk about Gregory Davis. It is a tragedy what happened to that young man. He had a promising future here at the bank. He was intelligent, a dogged investigator, and his mathematical and accounting skills were topnotch. It's a loss for us all." The words were appropriate, but the delivery was rote, leading to the conclusion that Stevens had had no emotional investment in Davis.

She pulled a small leather-bound notebook and a ballpoint pen from her bag. "Thank you for seeing me on such short notice, Mr. Stevens. What can you tell me about Mr. Davis? Did he have any enemies that you know of?"

"Enemies?" Stevens appeared surprised by the question. "Not that I know of. He was personable enough, and I've never heard a word spoken against him. He had only been with us a little over a year, and he was evidently highly recommended. He did not come in via the usual process. The bank's top management simply announced he would be working in this office, and he appeared one day for work. He was described as a forensic accountant. Other than that, I have no idea where he might have worked before, although he did speak with an accent. That's a little strange, of course, but there was nothing to complain about in his work. He was highly competent."

As Krystal's mother might have said, there was something 'off kilter' here. "You mean he didn't fill out an application?"

Stevens shook his head. "No. As I said, he was assigned to the position by the bank's management. It was a surprise to me."

"So, you have no paper on him, nothing about his background, maybe an application form?"

"Well," said Stevens, "everyone was sure he was Russian, of course, although he never referred to his origins one way or the other. He was pretty tight-lipped about it."

"You're telling me that a guy named Gregory Davis was Russian?"

"We didn't think that was his real name, or maybe he anglicized it when he immigrated. Wherever he came from, he was a hell of a forensic accountant."

"Can you tell me what he was working on at the time of his death?"

Stevens rubbed his chin. "Well, not really. First of all, there is bank confidentiality meant to protect our customers, and secondly our auditors work independently - it's the management style we've adopted."

Krystal was not sure she understood what this meant. "How about his computer? Is it possible to check what's on it?"

Stevens smiled condescendingly. "Same thing. We are bound by law to protect the confidentiality of our files. You would need a warrant to check any of them. But, none of our specialists have a single computer assigned to them. They don't even have individual cubicles. When they come to work, they can work at any station that happens to be open. Of course, there are what we call concentration rooms where they can go to discuss matters privately. Otherwise, it's a completely open floor."

This explanation was even more confusing. According to Stevens, the fourth largest bank in the United States permitted their employees to work on anything they liked and did not require them to report on what they were doing to management, presumably until they had reached a conclusion of some sort. She suspected there were a lot of coffee breaks during the workday. But she wasn't ready to give up just yet. "You mean there is no record at all of what Davis was working on at the time of his death? That just can't be."

"Oh, his work is stored in the central memory bank, of course. It's password protected, just like all the others."

"Have the police asked for access?"

"No, and I doubt they will. They just didn't seem too interested when they were here," he said breezily. "They only came around once." He glanced at his watch.

It seemed there was not much more Stevens could or would say. She thanked him for his time and was escorted back to the ground floor, her head churning with chaotic thoughts. The police had only paid what appeared to have been a perfunctory visit to Davis's place of employment? Presumably they also had spoken with his wife. They had concentrated all their efforts against Padruig Nessmith.

She walked from the bank back to the PSI offices mentally turning over what she had learned. Gregory Davis was a Russian just like his wife. So, she probably wasn't a mail-order bride as Strachey had speculated. But how was this relevant to his murder, if it was relevant, at all?

CHAPTER 9

Ruth Scatterfield was working on a new flower arrangement at the reception desk when Krystal returned. She looked up to greet her. "Afternoon, darlin'," she drawled. Krystal had a vision of her covered in syrup. "Y'all look worried."

Krystal did not appreciate being called 'darling' by anybody, but Ruth was a sweet person, and of an older generation, so she'd decided she could tolerate it. "Is Bob still in?" she asked.

"He's here," Ruth beamed and checked her watch. "It's about four o'clock, so I suppose he's just lit his pre-drink cigar. It'll soon be cocktail time."

Strachey had adopted the habit of inviting Krystal, Amy, and Ruth to his office for drinks in the afternoon. There was a wet bar discreetly installed inside a closet in his office to which he had the only key.

"We might need something to drink this afternoon," said Krystal.

"Oh?" Ruth's eyes grew large behind her glasses.

"Just had a strange meeting at the bank I have to tell him about."

She passed through the doors to the office spaces and found Strachey's door open. The aroma of an expensive cigar wafted into the hallway despite the special ventilation in his office ceiling. She thought of Captain Curry and his open window.

She poked her head through the door. "Can we talk, boss?"

Strachey looked up from a file folder on his desk and removed his reading glasses. The glasses were a recent addition to his wardrobe, and he didn't like people to see him wearing them. He didn't like the streaks of gray that were appearing in his hair either. His wife insisted it made him look distinguished, which was the last thing he wanted. He was in his shirtsleeves, cuffs rolled up and tie loosened.

Square jawed and tanned, he was a very handsome man, and he made the little girl who resided somewhere deep inside Krystal quiver just a bit when they were together.

She plopped into one of the chairs in front of his desk. "I just had a strange encounter with Davis's boss at the bank."

"You obviously can't wait to tell me about it," he smiled and drew on the Montecristo No. 2.

"Yeah, well, I didn't learn very much. His former boss says Davis was well-liked, an excellent worker with a future - a crackerjack forensic accountant, whatever that is. He worked in the Internal Audit Division. Unfortunately, his boss wouldn't or couldn't tell me anything about what he'd been working on. Seems they run a very loose ship over there, but the rules say they can't share client information. He said we'd need a warrant for that. But there's something else. It seems Davis was a Russian."

Strachey perked up. "Really? I would never have guessed that from his name. His wife being Russian now makes more sense, but I don't understand why Curry never mentioned it to us. What else did you find out about him?"

"Not much. His boss claims he has no information on his background. The bank's big bosses just announced one day that Davis would be working there, and he suddenly appeared."

Strachey chewed on this information for a moment, staring vaguely at the plume of blue smoke rising in a translucent column from the tip of his cigar.

"We should have a chat with Curry about this," he said. "I'll have Ruth set something up for tomorrow."

"You have an idea?"

"Maybe, but I want to check it out. There's something a little weird here."

"I agree. But what does it mean?"

"Maybe something, maybe everything, maybe nothing. The cops seem to have made up their minds that it was old Padruig."

CHAPTER 10

The Mecklenburg County Jail Central is a large, eight-story structure that cost about 150 million dollars to build so that Charlotte's criminals and suspected criminals could be boarded in style. Padruig Nessmith had been processed in the Arrest Processing Center where his fingerprints had been recorded electronically and a mugshot photo taken with modern, digital equipment, permitting the Deputy Sheriffs who ran the place to confirm beyond a doubt that he was, indeed, Padruig Nessmith. After processing, he was escorted next door to the jail which is located handily beside the court in Government Plaza. He was searched, issued an orange jumpsuit and placed in the pre-trial detention facility.

The morning following Padruig's arraignment Strachey, Krystal, and Holmes, again in a navy-blue suit and red tie, sat down with the prisoner in one of the facility's hospital-clean conference rooms. The prisoner was escorted into the room by a polite, bland-faced Deputy with long sideburns. She thought Padruig must be mortified by the out-sized jump suit and handcuffs, but he sat quietly, his face expressionless, where the Deputy placed him at the table before leaving the room and quietly closing the door.

There was an embarrassed silence before Holmes spoke. "Padruig, we need some facts."

Padruig sat very still with his eyes fixed on the tabletop. Several moments passed before he raised a taut face to Holmes and spoke. "The only fact you need to know is that I am innocent. My personal affairs are my business."

"Mr. Nessmith," Strachey said, "if we are to be of any use to you, at all, you are going to have to tell us everything. Why didn't you say you had left your house that day? The fact that you concealed that information only makes you look more guilty. Surely you can understand that."

Padruig swiveled his head to favor Strachey with a baleful look. "It is nobody's business what I do in my private life. I am not a murderer. That is all you need to know. This is nothing more than a witch hunt. The upper crust of Charlotte collectively don't like me because my family has not been here for two hundred years, and the rest don't like me because I'm rich. That's all there is to it. The whole thing is ridiculous. Your job is to get me out of here."

"Your attitude makes it very difficult for us to prove your innocence," Strachey shot back. "I'm not sure there is any more we can do."

Padruig considered this for a few beats then relented. "Very well. Yes, I left the house. I drove to Asheville to pick up my sister and bring her home. That's all there was to it."

"And there is nothing else we should know?"

"No." He lapsed into silence.

Holmes said he needed to speak with his client alone, and Strachey and Krystal walked out to the parking deck where they'd left Strachey's BMW.

Before they could get into the car, Holmes called to them from the door. They waited for him to catch up to them.

"I'm confident Padruig will be allowed out on bail. He should be home by afternoon."

"That's good news," said Strachey.

"Yes, it is. But his best hope resides in you, and whether he says so or not, I know he's counting on you. He's in a bad state."

"We're doing our best," replied Strachey, "but he's his own worst enemy."

Holmes nodded. "Yes, I know. I wish you luck."

As they drove away, leaving a forlorn Holmes in the rear-view mirror Strachey said, "You're going to have to talk to Padruig's sister."

"Gavenia? She gave me the silent treatment last time I was there."

"Well, she'll have no choice but to talk now. Can you go out there right now, before Padruig is cut loose? Maybe she'll tell you something useful."

"Oh, it'll be a treat," she said glumly. "What the hell is wrong with these people? Does Padruig have a death wish or something?"

"Beats the hell out of me."

"And what's with the names? Padruig? Gavenia?"

Strachey chuckled as he steered out of the parking garage and turned into the street. "They must be old Scots names. Remember, their father immigrated from Scotland."

"Humph. He didn't do his kids any favors there." She slumped in her seat

CHAPTER 11

Krystal used her cellphone to call ahead and warn Gavenia, and twenty minutes later pulled into the circular driveway in front of the Nessmith mansion. Gavenia must have been watching for her arrival because she opened the door even before Krystal had stepped onto the veranda. As before, she wore a dark dress that covered her ankles, and her hair was pulled back into a severe bun.

Gavenia was not an attractive woman, and Krystal could but wonder what she had been like when she was young. She had remained a spinster despite the undoubted attraction of her family's money. She was younger than Padruig, but it was hard to tell. A little make-up and more modern clothing would make a considerable difference. Did her older brother force the austerity on her because his own life was so devoid of color?

"Thank you for seeing me on such short notice, Miss Nessmith," began Krystal. "It's good to see you again."

As she drew near, she could see that Gavenia's eyes were shiny and rimmed in red. She had been crying. The realization that the woman must be frightened out of her mind slammed into Krystal with the force of a hurricane, and she was abruptly ashamed of her earlier derisiveness. Gently taking Gavenia's arm, she said, "Let's go inside and sit down."

Gavenia led her to a smaller, lighter room than the one in which she'd seen Padruig, a room that displayed a feminine touch with daintier furniture and oases of color. A vase of yellow roses sat on a table in front of a window, brightly limned by the afternoon sunlight.

Krystal felt unaccountably awkward with this strange, gray creature. "I'd like to talk a little bit about your brother," she ventured carefully.

Gavenia's lips quivered.

Krystal rushed ahead. "You understand we're trying to help him, don't you? We're looking for any information, no matter how little, that will help exonerate him."

"I need him here at home," said Gavenia with an effort. She gulped back a sob.

"I understand." Krystal noticed the silence that had settled over the house. "Are you alone here, Gavenia? May I call you Gavenia?"

The older woman nodded. "We have a cleaning service here twice a week, but I do all the cooking."

With the family's wealth, permanent house staff was well within their reach. "Is there anyone who can be with you? Anyone you can talk to? A friend?"

Gavenia shook her head again, and it evoked an emotion in Krystal that she only rarely felt - pity. She wanted to help this woman, but she didn't know how it could be done save a miracle. "The police discovered that Padruig was away from home the day of the murders. He was seen in his car not far from where it happened. He told us this morning that he drove to Asheville to fetch you. Is that true?"

Gavenia swallowed another sob and said, "Yes, I had spent the night at the home there. He picked me up and drove me back here."

Krystal was curious. "You have a second house

in Asheville?"

"Oh, it's not like that." She brightened for a second. "It's a home for girls in need, pregnant girls and unwed mothers. It's connected with our church, St. Ann. We're Catholic, you know."

No, she didn't know. Krystal was uncertain she had heard correctly. "You spent the night in a home for unwed mothers?"

Gavenia ventured a wan smile. "Yes, that's right. I'm there quite frequently."

This was an unexpected tangent, but Krystal decided to follow it. "Why is that, Gavenia?"

The older woman gave Krystal an anxious look. "I'm not sure I should say."

Krystal inwardly cursed the reticence of the Nessmiths. It must be a familial trait, and it was maddening. "Gavenia, any information you have could help your brother."

Gavenia thought about this as though she were pondering whether to reveal an atomic secret. "Very well," she said at last, "the house used to be our family's summer home, but we signed it over to the Church. The home is associated with St. Ann, but Padruig provides all the funding. He's done so for years. My visits there are simply to check on the girls and comfort them as best I can."

If Gavenia had said her brother was from Mars and the mother ship had landed in Asheville Krystal could not have been more astonished. Padruig Nessmith financed a home for unwed mothers? Of all the things she might think of the close-mouthed curmudgeon, philanthropy was the farthest from what she would have expected. "Er," she began uncertainly, "how long have you been doing this?"

"Oh," said Gavenia, brightening a bit, "for many years now. We've always done all we can to help the Church. Padruig also helps fund the church school and other activities."

"Do many people know about this?"

Gavenia was taken aback. "Oh, my, no. Padruig would never permit it. And he never attends services. He only drives me there for Mass." She paused for a moment, "Of course, the Diocese and Father Timothy at St. Ann are aware."

"Why doesn't your brother want his charitable activities to be public?" *It would go a long way to improving his image.*

Gavenia leaned toward her and lowered her voice to a reverent whisper, "The Bible tells us, 'Take heed that you do not your alms before men, to be seen of them: otherwise you have no reward of your Father which is in Heaven.' Padruig is not a vain man."

As Krystal digested this, Gavenia smiled beatifically and closed her eyes. Krystal could have sworn she was praying. The Bible verse seemed to have buoyed her spirits.

"Um," Krystal continued, "on the day in question, what time did Padruig pick you up in Asheville?"

Gavenia's brow wrinkled in thought, then she nodded to herself and said, "It was about 2:30 in the afternoon. I'm certain of it, because we had had lunch with the girls, and I spent some time afterwards with Sylvia, a sweet little thing from Raleigh. She has a little baby girl."

*****

A half-hour later Krystal pulled into the street and headed for PSI as a new image of Padruig Nessmith took shape in her mind. Could he really be Padruig the Pious? His secret charities were in sharp contrast to his public image, an image he was at pains to maintain even to the point of public condemnation. The wealthy more often than not were anything but reticent to trumpet their good works, but not in this case. The hurt and humiliation he had suffered had driven him inside himself where he felt safe from the world, and Gavenia's revelations suggested he wanted to protect the weakest among us from similar pain. Perhaps she and Strachey had misjudged the man, though Padruig had not helped his cause. What a strange creature he was.

CHAPTER 12

Krystal chewed her lower lip. She'd walked into Strachey's office with a frown on her face.

"What's up now?" He asked. He was smoking an early cigar, a short one from which he'd removed the band, and there was a mug of coffee near his hand.

She sank into a chair and shook her head. She'd done a lot of thinking on the drive back to the office. "You know," she said, "maybe everybody has old Padruig wrong. Like your aunt Sadie said, Christanna jilted him over twenty years ago. Crimes of passion are usually committed by young people, but Padruig's response was not rage. He just retreated into a shell like a hermit crab into a tin can and never came out. If he was going to go after his brother and Christanna, it would have been more natural to have done it back then. Everybody thinks he's an old curmudgeon with no human feelings, but just the opposite may be true."

Strachey had no idea where she was going with this. "What do you mean?"

She told him about her conversation with Gavenia, then said, "Instead of a cold, calculating, cruel person, it's more likely he's a wounded soul who has decided he can't cope with human society because he believes he will be betrayed at every turn. Looking at the facts, can we really subscribe to the 'revenge is a dish best served cold' theory the police and everyone else have adopted? Is it reasonable to believe that his anger took over twenty years to get hot enough to commit murder? That would have been a really slow burn, but it's what people seem willing to believe."

Strachey took a long drag from his cigar, which by now had burned down to half its original length. He stood from behind his desk, head wreathed in smoke, and went to the closet door which he opened with a key to access the bar. "I think we can start happy hour a few minutes early today. Scotch OK with you?"

She hesitated, then smirked. "You don't have anything else in here, do you?"

"Oh, there are a couple more things, but I don't understand how anyone could wish to drink anything else." He measured a finger of Laphroaig single malt into two glasses, added a few drops of water to each, and handed her a glass before returning to his desk and taking a contemplative sip.

"I think you may be onto something," he said after a moment. Can you take it a little further?"

She swirled the amber liquid in her glass, reluctant to drink it, as she organized her thoughts. "Okay. Murder usually has a more immediate motive. Often murder is committed without a plan in a single moment of rage - crimes of passion. Sure, being left standing at the altar had to have been a traumatic, psychologically scarring event. But has Padruig ever exhibited violence toward anyone? Not that we've been able to find out. No, his defense has been to retreat from the world, find a dark corner where he could feel safe and comfortable. Such behavior does not suggest a violent or murder-prone individual. Quite the opposite, in fact. Padruig has the soul of a sheep rather than a wolf."

Strachey drained his glass and grinned. "Damn, Krystal, that was almost poetic. So, you're saying that Padruig should be the last rather than the first person anyone should suspect of murder."

She finally took a small sip of the pungent, smoky whisky. "That's exactly what I said. The question, then, is if Padruig isn't the killer, who would have shot his brother and sister-in-law and why? None of my inquiries turned up an enemy. They were universally liked."

She could see that Strachey was warming to her theory. "Right. Maybe everybody is looking at this the wrong way. Maybe Jaidon and Christanna were not the targets of the killer, after all. Maybe it was the bank guy, Davis, or whatever his real name was."

Krystal frowned. "I don't understand why the police haven't come up with the same idea. Davis' boss said Curry's people had visited the bank only once."

"That makes it even more important to talk to Curry again. Something smells here, and what the bank guy told you leads me to suspect where it's coming from. I'll have Ruth set up another meeting for us."

"What are you thinking?"

"Let's wait and talk to Curry first. That will tell us something one way or another."

Strachey was talking like a spook again, and it made her feel excluded. As her partner, even if she was just a salaried partner, he should share everything with her, but she knew she could not overcome the ex-CIA operative's ingrained habits. She would just have to wait.

CHAPTER 13

Captain Curry agreed to meet them the next afternoon, and they drove to police headquarters in Strachey's BMW. He parked in the lot behind the building, and they started walking around to the front entrance. As they turned onto the sidewalk Strachey grabbed Krystal's arm and pulled her back behind the corner.

Startled, she asked, "What's going on?"

He peeked around the corner toward the front entrance before moving them farther back into the shadow. "Quick," he said, "we've got to get out of sight." She was puzzled but followed him at a trot back to the parking lot where they tumbled into his car. "Hunch down," he said, staring hard through the steering wheel out the windshield.

She followed his gaze in time to see two men in dark suits round the corner and walk into the lot deep in conversation. They got into a black Chevy Suburban two rows away. Strachey straightened in his seat as the Suburban pulled away. "Well," he murmured, "I'll be damned."

Krystal was mystified. "What the hell was that?" she asked.

Strachey's expression was hard to read. "You saw those guys in the Suburban?"

"Of course, I saw them. You know who they were?"

"I know one of them." He sat silently for a moment, chewing on his thoughts, which exasperated Krystal.

"Well, damn it, are you going to tell me, or are you going to keep me in the dark. You're acting too damned spooky."

This made him smile, and he relaxed his shoulders back into the seat. "The one I recognized is an old CIA colleague from the Russia House."

"The 'Russia House?'"

"It's what they're calling the old Soviet Division these days. I think they've been watching too many movies out there at Langley. It's a stupidly dramatic name."

This was the last thing she expected or welcomed. "The fucking CIA? What the hell are they doing here?"

"Think about it," he said, ignoring the slur on his old outfit. "You discovered that Gregory Davis was a Russian. Today we see a CIA Russian ops type at police headquarters. Seems a little too coincidental to ignore, don't you think?"

"The fucking CIA," she repeated. "Why is it that every time I get involved in a case the damned spooks or the FBI show up? It's like a curse."

He laughed out loud at this. "I think it's a road to Damascus moment in this case and maybe the key to everything."

"Explain."

"Let's go talk to Curry first. That should give us a clue."

"You're still being spooky with me, and I don't like it." She crossed her arms and had no intention of moving until Strachey came clean about what he was thinking.

"Look," he said, "what I'm thinking will be

confirmed or disproved by what Curry says. I don't want to prejudice your thinking until I'm certain. One of us must remain unbiased until we have some facts. I'm sorry, but that's the way it is. It's the way I've always worked."

Krystal was doing a slow burn. "Damn it, Bob. You're not in the CIA anymore, and I'm your partner, or so you say. In my world, partners share everything."

She could tell she was making him uncomfortable, and it gave her a small tingle of satisfaction. He needed to realize he wasn't working for the government these days. He was in a different world when it came to criminal investigation, and it was her world where her experience was more relevant.

He clinched his jaw, but then relaxed. "OK, you're right. Here it is. I think the Agency is involved somehow with Gregory Davis. I think he might have been a defector. That would explain why he showed up a year ago and was given a position at the bank out of the blue. It's the way the Agency works when it resettles a defector. They give him a new name, find him a job that suits his abilities, buy him a house, and so on. What this means for the investigation, I don't know … yet. It's going to require some more digging, and I doubt the Agency will cooperate."

"It's definitely a curse," she moaned. But she was gratified to have brought Strachey around.

"Ready to see Curry?" he asked.

"Let's go."

*****

Captain Abel Curry was not especially pleased to see them. In fact, he looked worried, and there was a thin sheen of sweat on his shaved pate. He invited them to be seated after shaking hands. "What can I do for you today?" he asked without a trace of enthusiasm.

Strachey did the talking. "Well, Captain, we've been looking into different aspects of the case. Yesterday, Krystal interviewed Gregory Davis's boss at the bank and uncovered an interesting fact. Davis was a Russian. He appeared at the bank about a year ago and was given a job in the Internal Audit Division with no questions asked. His boss knew nothing about his background. Apparently, he was an excellent worker and got on well with everyone. We tried to interview his widow, but she refused to talk to us, which we found a little strange. It was as though she had been instructed to say nothing to anybody. We were wondering what you thought about Davis. You didn't mention to us that he was Russian."

Curry arranged his features into a semblance of studied neutrality. "I don't see how any of that is relevant to the investigation. Padruig Nessmith is the prime suspect, and we know he had motive. Davis was just in the wrong place at the wrong time."

Strachey watched the Captain carefully with eyes long trained to know when someone was lying. "We're beginning to think it's possible that Davis was the killer's real target and the Nessmiths were the ones in the wrong place at the wrong time."

Curry squirmed a bit in his chair. "I don't think so," he said. "As you know, Padruig Nessmith is likely to be charged with first degree murder in a few weeks despite the judge letting him out on bail. The matter is nearly closed."

Strachey persisted. "Is there anything more you can tell us about Davis? Why won't his widow talk to us?"

"It's her prerogative to speak or not to speak with whomever she pleases," said Curry, not bothering to disguise his irritation. "I have nothing more to say on the matter."

"I see," said Strachey. "Well, that sounds pretty conclusive. Just one more question, if you don't mind, Captain. What were you talking about with the CIA today?"

Curry's façade of neutrality crumbled entirely, and his face turned red. "I don't know what you're talking about, Strachey. This meeting is over."

The Captain stood to signal they should leave. Strachey turned back at the door and said, "Thanks again, Captain. I think you've told us everything we need to know."

They left Curry standing open-mouthed behind his desk.

In the hallway Strachey laughed out loud. "Well, I'll be damned. We're on the right track now for sure. He was lying through his teeth. Did you see his reaction when I mentioned the CIA?"

"Couldn't miss it," she answered. "What do you think it means?"

"It means there is a lot more going on than meets the eye."

"We're not going to get anything more out of Curry, though," she said.

"You're right about that. He's one of those people easily impressed with Federal credentials. He's been instructed to keep his mouth shut, and he's going to obey orders. We need to find out why because there is something more than an open and shut murder case going on here."

Back in the car, Krystal asked, "Do you think you can find out anything from your old CIA contacts?"

"That would be problematic, I think. I've been out of the business for a long while now, and Amy's left the Agency, too. The guy I recognized back there is Tony DeLorenzo. We had a passing acquaintance back in the day. He's a good officer and should have made senior grade by now. I guess I could try to get in touch with him directly and try to keep it off the books. But I think it's likely he won't be willing or able to tell me anything."

She had an idea but was reluctant to say it out loud. After a long silence, she said, "You know I have a good contact in the FBI."

He turned toward her. "You mean Enoch Whitehall."

"Yeah."

"He's the Executive Assistant Director for Counterintelligence."

"Right again."

"Pretty powerful guy."

"He's another damned spook legend, but he's always been good to me."

"Don't I know it," he said. Whitehall had literally saved Krystal's life a year earlier when she had been held prisoner by a mad man on Maryland's Eastern Shore. "But I'm not sure he could help. DeLorenzo is CIA."

"Whitehall has good contacts at the Agency, and how about the guy DeLorenzo was with? Could he have been FBI? CIA doesn't operate inside the States, does it?" She wasn't so sure about where and how the CIA really operated.

"I guess it could have been the FBI. And if it was, it would have been counterintelligence. That's Whitehall's bailiwick."

"So, should I call him?"

Strachey thought about this. "I don't think so. He's too cagey to say anything over the phone. You'll have to go to Washington."

"Shit." She hated the idea.

"It's the only way we'll get anything out of him," persisted Strachey, and with a sinking feeling she knew he was right. She began to wish she'd never mentioned Whitehall.

"We might not get anything out of him even if I go to Washington," she ventured.

"Do you think it's worth a try?"

"I guess it can't hurt," she answered reluctantly, surrendering at last. "Christ, I hate the idea of going back to Washington. It's full of crazy people."

Strachey couldn't restrain a chuckle at this. "I can't argue with you there but think about it."

"Okay," she said, and a cloud of gloom settled over her.

CHAPTER 14

Strachey insisted that she fly to Washington rather than drive. It was a short flight, which only intensified her dread of returning there. She viewed Washington and its environs as populated by busy people, each and every one of whom believed he or she and the government institution they worked for was the absolute center of the universe. The self-importance of government bureaucrats never failed to amaze her.

The plane descended along the Potomac River, and she could see the city with its alabaster monuments slide by on the left side of the aircraft until the water of the river rose up to fill the window as they landed at Reagan National Airport. She picked up her rental car and threaded her way out of the airport onto the George Washington Memorial Parkway, heading north. Within minutes she was on the 14th Street Bridge which took her across the top of the National Mall, with the Smithsonian buildings stretched away to her right and the Washington Monument towering on her left. Soon enough she turned east onto Constitution Avenue hoping to find a spot to park. Naturally, she failed.

It was late morning, and it was summer, which in Washington meant the humidity was high and the heat sweltering, driving the city's denizens to madness or to seek out air-conditioned refuge wherever they could find it. Only the tourists braved the heat. Krystal's mood was not improved by at last finding an open parking space on the Mall six blocks from the FBI building. The trek to Pennsylvania Avenue convinced her she would have been no less comfortable in the

Mojave Desert. Funny thing about heat. There is wet heat, like now in Washington, and dry heat like in Spain, which Strachey assured her was very pleasant. She had found the heat even in Miami compared favorably to that in Washington, something she attributed to the easy-going culture of Miami compared to the rat race, with literal rats, in the nation's capital.

Having arrived at the crumbling facade of the J. Edgar Hoover building a scant five minutes before time for her appointment with Enoch Whitehall, she was ashamed of how grateful she was for the air conditioning. Not for the first time she was escorted to Whitehall's office by a somber young man dressed in a dark suit, white shirt, and conservative tie. He was wearing wingtips, too, probably hoping that his emulation would win him a junior man in black badge someday. He opened the door so she could enter the antechamber, guarded as always by a stern woman of indeterminate age. Krystal thought of her as the dragon guarding Whitehall's lair, and the only thing she knew about her was that her name was Jeanne, although she would never have dared to call her by name.

"Good morning, Miss Murphy. Right on time, I see." Jeanne greeted her in a crisp formal voice while her eyes examined her as if to determine whether she met the standard required to meet with Whitehall. "Please take a seat. The Director will be with you in a moment."

About ten minutes later, Jeanne stood from behind her behemoth desk and announced, "The Director will see you now." She held open the heavy wooden door that led to the inner chamber. Whitehall's office was notable for its total lack of personality. There was not one object in the room that was not government issue, and the only decoration was a framed photograph on the wall behind the desk of a younger Whitehall shaking hands with J. Edgar Hoover. Hoover was smiling up at the taller Whitehall whose face somehow gave an impression of pleasure without smiling. Not for the first time, she wondered how old Whitehall was.

She found him standing behind his desk to greet her, thin, bony hand extended, and once again she wondered at the nearly phantasmic impression he gave. His normal dark suit, charcoal she thought, hung a bit more loosely from his cadaverous frame than she remembered, and his hatchet face, dominated by a blade of a nose seemed ever so little gaunter. The intensity of his gray eyes, however, had not diminished, and now they surveyed her with benevolent curiosity.

He invited her to take a seat in one of the wooden chairs that faced his desk and said, "It's a pleasure to see you again, Krystal, but an unexpected pleasure. What brings you back to Washington?"

She was almost embarrassed to admit that she had come once again seeking a favor. "We're working on a case in Charlotte," she began, "and we seem to have run into an official roadblock."

"In Charlotte." He said in a neutral voice, as if confirming a fact.

"Um, yes. Strachey thinks we've run into a CIA stonewall of some kind concerning a Russian named Gregory Davis."

Whitehall went still for a moment staring at her, his eyes nictating like some reptile as a mask of detachment slipped over his face. At that moment Krystal remembered that this legendary and mysterious man was a powerful denizen of the most profound depths of the Washington swamp. As a swamp creature of the first order, his first loyalty was to the swamp and its many secrets. Her spirit sagged with the realization that it had been a mistake to come here.

Finally, Whitehall spoke, and his voice was cold and precise. "I'm afraid I can't help you."

Krystal had not expected much would be gained by this trip, but she had not anticipated provoking Whitehall's hostility. Foolishly, as she later realized, she gave it one more try. "Do you mean it is a CIA matter, and the FBI can do nothing?"

"As I said, I can't help you," he repeated in a voice cold enough to drain all the warmth from the room. He rose abruptly to his feet. "I'm afraid I have no more time, Miss Murphy. So, if you will please excuse me ..."

Krystal could not help but notice the switch from "Krystal" to "Miss Murphy." She stood and said, "I'm sorry to have bothered you with this. Thanks for your time."

"Goodbye, Miss Murphy." Whitehall did not offer his hand in farewell.

Jeanne the dragon summoned another escort who led her to the exit and retrieved her visitor's badge. The long, debilitating walk back to her rental car did nothing to improve her mood. By the time she had the engine running and the air blasting, she was angry. Angry with herself, angry with Strachey, and angry with Whitehall. In fact, she was angry at the world. She was unkind to other drivers on the way back to Reagan National, liberally using her horn and weaving in and out of traffic. She sat sullenly on the rental company's shuttle bus as the driver waited for other passengers, mentally cursing Russians, the CIA and the FBI, as well as the Charlotte police and Bob Strachey. She wanted a drink badly, but that would have to wait until she was back in Charlotte. She hated the idea that Whitehall would think of her as the sort of person who came whining to him for help every time she ran into a problem. More importantly, she worried that she may have blotted her copybook permanently with the man who had been a powerful ally in the past.

*****

When Murphy was gone, the FBI's Executive Director for Counterintelligence rose from behind his desk and walked slowly to the window which looked out over Pennsylvania Avenue and stood there, deep in thought, oblivious to the busy street below. He reached a decision and returned to his desk where he lifted the receiver from its cradle and pushed a button. "Jeanne," he said, "would you please get the Deputy Director for Operations of the Central Intelligence Agency on the secure line?"

*****

"So, he went cold and clammed up when you mentioned Gregory Davis?" Strachey leaned back and swirled the whisky in his glass. He'd invited Krystal to join him in enjoying the 10-year-old Talisker, but she declined. As much as she was tempted after the difficult day, she was only too aware of her weakness for alcohol.

"Yeah. The portcullis came crashing down and

the drawbridge was pulled up as soon as I mentioned him. It was an amazing thing to see, almost like a physical transformation. It was clear that I'd stepped over some line. I should never have gone to Washington."

Strachey took a contemplative sip of the Talisker and gave his glass a complimentary nod. "I dunno, Krystal. Could be, you've confirmed my suspicions. Whitehall's reaction suggests he knows what's going on."

"And what good does that do us or Padruig?"

"Well, we know more now than we did before."

"I repeat, what good does it do us?"

"If I'm reading things right, Whitehall's reaction confirms what we suspected. There's something fishy about Gregory Davis, and the Government guys are up to their necks in it. The trick now is to find out what's really going on and how Padruig fits in."

"You think Padruig is involved with the CIA?" Krystal was incredulous.

"No, of course not, but he has a role in whatever's going on. I just can't figure out what it is."

This was not especially comforting.

CHAPTER 15

Most Saturday mornings Strachey liked to laze around the house, drink a lot of strong, black coffee and catch up on the newspapers. He was often interrupted by six-year-old Robert Thomas who enjoyed running at full tilt through the house with a beach towel tied around his neck shouting "I'm Thor." A large wooden spoon served as Thor's magic hammer, and it had taken considerable effort to convince him not to throw it in the house. Robert Thomas's behavior was not improved by the attitude of his maternal grandfather, Thomas Jefferson Dawson, who delighted in almost anything his grandson did. Strachey's wife, Amy, was out on her morning five-mile run.

Robert and Amy enjoyed their new more laid-back life in the slower pace of Charlotte. She had been reluctant to leave her work at the CIA but in the end was persuaded by both her husband and her father that Charlotte would provide a better environment for Robert Thomas than the frenetic suburbs of Washington. She did some work at PSI, putting her ability to navigate the Internet to good use, although background checks were mere child's play compared to what she had been doing at the Agency. The bottom line was that she had more time to spend with Robert Thomas who was now in the First Grade at Charlotte Country Day School and enjoying it greatly.

"Thomas," said Strachey, "why don't you take this hellion out to the back yard where he can throw his 'hammer.' With any luck, you're slow enough these days for him to hit you."

Thomas Jefferson twisted his mobile mahogany face into a mock frown. "I ain't slowed down that much."

Always on the alert to be helpful, Robert Thomas piped, "You shouldn't say 'ain't,' Papaw. It's bad grammar."

Thomas Jefferson beamed, "Now ain't that my smart little boy. I guess that fancy school's good for something. C'mon, let's go out back and play like your papa says. I'll give you a run for it."

Strachey chuckled. He had to admit the old boy was still pretty spry.

When they were gone, he settled back into the chair and unfolded the paper again. He was half-way through an article about the upcoming golf tournament at Quail Hollow when the phone rang. To answer he would be forced stand up and walk across the room. He considered just letting it ring, but then got up, thinking it might be Krystal. But he didn't recognize the number from the caller i.d. and again considered not answering. If it was important, the caller could leave a message. But he was already out of his comfortable chair standing beside the phone. He lifted the receiver. "Hello."

A man's voice emerged from the earpiece. "Is this Robert Strachey?"

He thought it must be a telemarketer. "Who's calling, please?"

"I'm going to assume you are Robert Strachey," the man said. "This is Tony DeLorenzo, Bob. Do you remember me?"

Of course, he remembered DeLorenzo. He'd worked with him a few times at the Agency. More importantly, he was one of the two men they'd spotted leaving police headquarters the other day, the one from Russia House. No one from the Agency had contacted him in years, and it felt a little strange, but when he thought about it, it was not entirely unexpected. "Sure, Tony, I remember you. Why are you calling?"

"We need to talk."

"About what? I don't have anything to do with the Agency anymore."

"It's not something we can discuss on the phone. I know you're retired, or quit, or whatever you did, but I hope you still feel some loyalty to the outfit."

"That depends on what the outfit is doing."

Frustration, or maybe it was urgency, colored DeLorenzo"s voice. "Look, Bob, can we meet and talk, or what?"

Strachey said nothing for several beats, enjoying the idea of increasing DeLorenzo's anxiety. "Sure, Tony, we can meet. Where and when did you have in mind?"

"You know this town better than me. I'll go anywhere you say."

"Where are you staying?"

"Embassy Suites, uptown."

"They have a bar, don't they?"

"Yes, of course."

"I'll meet you there at one o'clock."

"Thanks, Bob. See you at one."

Strachey replaced the receiver and stood there tapping his foot as he thought. Whatever DeLorenzo wanted to talk about related to the Padruig Nessmith case, he had no doubt, but he suspected it had more to do with Gregory Davis. He thought about calling Krystal with the news but decided to wait. Krystal had a weekend guest, her boyfriend from Miami, and he saw no reason to disturb their weekend until he knew more.

Embassy Suites Uptown had been open only a few months. The bar was a modern affair with bottles displayed in lighted glass cases and a strange, green glow surrounding the bar itself. DeLorenzo was easy to spot as no one else was in the place. He'd selected a stool at the end of the bar near the floor to ceiling windows. The spook was wearing a dark suit with no tie, and when he saw Strachey he stood and produced a welcoming smile, the kind of smile old comrades offer when seeing one another after a long absence. "Hi, Bob, it's sure good to see you again. I couldn't believe you'd gone into the private security business down here. How're Amy and your boy?"

Strachey reciprocated the smile and answered, "Everybody's fine, Tony." DeLorenzo was doing what the Agency referred to as 'establishing rapport.' "Charlotte is almost my hometown, you know, and it's nice to be away from Washington and the Beltway."

They both mounted barstools. Strachey glanced around and said, "I don't see a bartender."

"Yeah," nodded DeLorenzo, "sorry about that. The bar doesn't open until four. I forgot."

"Well," said Strachey, "that should suit us just fine. Enough small talk; what do you want?"

DeLorenzo lost his smile at Strachey's directness. "I understand you have a nosy female ex-cop working for you, someone known to rock the boat."

Strachey hid his surprise. Why would the CIA have its sights on Krystal? "And ...?"

"And, we want you to keep her on a leash."

"'We' being ... ?"

"The Agency and the FBI."

"And why would I want to do this, Tony?"

DeLorenzo reached into his jacket pocket and withdrew a sheet of paper which he unfolded and laid in front of Strachey. The document was familiar; it was a standard government confidentiality agreement.

"What's this?"

DeLorenzo's adopted an official mien. "You know what it is, Bob. What I'm about to tell you is highly confidential information that must be protected."

Strachey shoved the paper back to DeLorenzo. "I'm not going to sign anything." He resented the Agency's assumption that they still had some sort of hold over him and decided to push back.

"It's important, Bob."

"I don't care. I'm not going to sign it, and if that ends our conversation, so be it." He started to stand up, but DeLorenzo placed a hand on his arm.

"Come on, Bob," he said, "you know how these things work. It's standard fare."

"Maybe for you, Tony, but not for me. I'm not in the secrecy business any longer. I'm a private citizen running a private business, and I don't need any of your secrets to do my job." Strachey suspected the document was a ploy; if he signed it, great, if he didn't DeLorenzo probably had another option. He wondered what it might be.

Something in Strachey's voice convinced DeLorenzo that it was a lost cause. "I'm sorry you feel that way, but it doesn't change anything. We want you to stand down on the Nessmith case."

What would he do, he wondered, if he were dependent on a government pension that someone like

DeLorenzo could snatch away?   Fortunately, he was now independently wealthy.   "Padruig Nessmith has nothing to do with the government. He's my client, and I most certainly will not abandon him. If you have some information you think I need to know, you'd better spill it now because, if not, we won't be seeing one another again." He stared hard at the spook.

DeLorenzo caught the incipient anger in Strachey's eyes and silently retrieved the unsigned confidentiality agreement from the bar and replaced it in his pocket with a heavy sigh. "Well, it was worth a try," he said with a wry smile.

Strachey relaxed and essayed a shot across the bow.   "This isn't about Padruig Nessmith, is it?   It's about Gregory Davis."

DeLorenzo pulled a long face, then gave Strachey a lopsided grin. "You're smarter than the average bear, Bob."

Strachey leaned forward, his elbow on the bar. "Who is he, Tony, a defector?"

"So, you figured that out, did you?"

Strachey waited.

DeLorenzo heaved another heavy sigh and continued, "His real name is Grigoriy Pushkin. He kept the books for a very important oligarch who is close to Putin. The mistake the oligarch made was to hire an honest man. After a year moving the guy's ill-gotten money around the world, Grigoriy defected with his wife, and the result was major damage to the Russians' illegal financial network.   You've seen what the Russians are up to these days with defectors ..."

A light bulb went on. "You mean you think this was a Russian hit on a defector, like in the UK?"

DeLorenzo nodded. "That's what the FBI thinks. There has been some clandestine reporting about Russian illegals in the States. No one in Washington wants the bad publicity that would appear if we started having people killed in America the way they have been in the UK. It would mean a real shit storm, and the FBI has been taking a lot of hits lately. They're desperate to keep a lid on this."

"At the expense of Padruig Nessmith." Strachey got a bad taste in his mouth.

The CIA man nodded again. "If needs be. It's good cover. Matter of national security. Nessmith's arrest was just to make the Russians think they can relax."

Strachey was doing a slow burn. "So, in the interests of national security the government is willing to sacrifice an innocent man?"

DeLorenzo had the grace to look sheepish. "Until the real killers are in custody, anyway. That's our plan. The FBI has mounted a massive manhunt all over the Southeast."

"But you've shared the stuff about the illegals with the police?" Strachey already knew the answer.

DeLorenzo spread his arms. "You know how local cops are. Captain Curry's not buying it entirely. He's garnered too much good publicity by arresting the prime suspect. He doesn't want to give away his prize. But he is cooperating."

"And you guys won't permit any publicity about the possible Russian connection."

"The FBI sure as hell won't. If there's a leak, they'll throw a big hissy fit, and woe to the leaker."

"Speaking of the FBI, what exactly motivated you

to have this friendly chat with me?   '

"It's about your girl," said DeLorenzo. "She paid a visit to the Bureau's Deputy Director for Counterintelligence, and it set off alarm bells. Seems like she has a certain reputation in Washington. Phone calls were made. Discussions were held. Shit hit the fan. And someone had the idea we should ask you for help."

This was logical. Washington counted on old loyalties to insure people kept their mouths shut. Trouble was, Strachey had never considered himself an old boy, and he wondered how Krystal would react to someone calling her his 'girl.' "What do you think about this Russian illegal idea?" he asked.

"Like I said, it's an FBI thing," said DeLorenzo. "The reporting has been vague. If you've been reading the papers, you know we're short on inside sources these days. But the feebies have the bit between their teeth. It's really their game."

"Seems like it could be a wild goose chase."

"Well, then," said DeLorenzo, "that would put the ball right back in your client's court, wouldn't it. Seems to me you should be hoping the Bureau is right and they bring the assassin to ground."

He had a point. As fantastical as the Russian assassin idea sounded, it did offer hope to clear Padruig despite Curry's obstinacy.

Strachey stood. "Thanks, Tony. You'll let me know if anything turns up?"

"Sure."

Strachey didn't believe him.

CHAPTER 16

Monday morning's sky was threatened by a distant procession of slowly moving dark-rimmed clouds promising some rain to temper the summer warmth of the Queen City. But they were no match for the storm clouds that swirled through Krystal's thoughts. She arrived at the PSI offices just before noon, having come straight from the airport where she'd dropped Ray Velazquez to catch his flight back to Miami. Strachey had been waiting impatiently to tell her his news but must have seen that something was off with her as soon as she walked into his office. "Hey, kid, are you OK?"

She sank into the chair in front of his desk and laid her head back to face the ceiling. Strachey remained silent. Finally, she raised her head, took a deep breath, and brought her hazel eyes to focus on him. "I'm OK," she said, her voice unusually soft as though she were speaking from a great distance. "What's up. Ruth said you wanted to see me."

Strachey's concern could be read on his face, but he evidently decided not to probe, for which she was grateful. He said, "Um, yes. It appears that your visit to Washington stirred things up."

With an effort she turned her thoughts to the non-productive meeting with Enoch Whitehall. The only thing she remembered stirring up was the quick brush-off he'd given her. It had disturbed her at the time. Whitehall had never acted like that in the past. In fact, he'd been more than friendly and almost always helpful. She worried that she had spoiled their friendship. "What do you mean 'stirred things up?'"

"It turns out that you have a reputation in certain circles in Washington. It's not a bad reputation, as far as I'm concerned, but it's the kind that make people nervous because they can't predict what you'll do. It's one of the things I like about you, as a matter of fact."

"Uh-huh." She was having a hard time concentrating on what Strachey was saying. "Listen, Bob, could we talk later? I have some things to think about."

"Um, sure. Take all the time you want."

She wanted to push the events of the weekend out of her mind but was helpless to do so. Ray Velazquez's visit had been a disaster from beginning to end, and by the time she dropped him at the airport that morning she was feeling uncharacteristically fragile. She'd invited him to visit her in her new digs in Charlotte, and he'd agreed. She'd hoped he would be enthusiastic about her improved lifestyle and that it would somehow give a lift to their flagging relationship. But when she picked him up at the airport his mood was anything but enthusiastic. His embrace was light, and a perfunctory peck on the cheek replaced their usual passionate reunion.

Their long-distance romance had survived five years now, but with each passing day, Ray grew more dissatisfied. If Krystal was not happy in Arlington, why wouldn't she move to Miami where a position in the Dade County Police was all but guaranteed? But now, when she finally was leaving Arlington, it was to move to North Carolina.

"I just can't understand why you're doing this.

You're throwing away a career you've spent years building, and you know you could easily transfer down to Miami and work with me. But North Carolina?"

His attitude was not improved by Krystal's response. "I'm making three times what I did as a cop, Ray, more than I could make here in Miami, too. What's so hard to understand?"

She had spoken in haste and instantly regretted it. Ray's problem was not what she was doing, but where she was doing it.

She tried again. "I liked being a cop, Ray, but in the end, there was just too much bureaucracy for me. It was just too frustrating. And if I came to work with Dade County down here, it would just be jumping from one bureaucracy to another."

"But why North Carolina?" he persisted.

"Because I'll be working with Bob Strachey who is as far from a bureaucrat as you can get. We work well together, and he respects me."

"So, you like Strachey, do you?"

"He's a married man, Ray, and his wife is my best friend."

"But you're still just an employee."

This raised her hackles again. "Much closer to partner than employee," she shot back. Despite her protestations she could not escape a feeling of guilt. Her first serious relationship in years was slipping through her fingers.

Total dedication to the job had long ago pushed any hope of a normal life into a tiny, dusty corner, maybe into a closet. Ray Velazquez had changed all of that, and she had known real joy with him, the kind of comfort with another that had been rare, nearly nonexistent, in her life. Now she was losing it. She was accustomed to facing facts and acting accordingly. Decisions must be made, but right now she wanted to push them as far as possible into the future, but she couldn't.

Ray had come to issue an ultimatum - either she come to live with him in Miami, or the relationship was over. It was a stark choice, and they debated it for two days and nights, interspersed with bouts of glum silence. Ray slept on the sofa.

Nothing she said would change his mind, and as he rebuffed every idea, she could feel the anger smoldering inside and fought to repress it. Her "Irish" would do her no good in this instance.

She could not bring herself to submit to his demand and hated herself for it, suspecting her reaction was somehow perverse.   Was his ultimatum so unreasonable, after all? He wanted something more permanent, marriage, children. Maybe it was some sort of Hispanic thing. But she could not see herself in that role as much as she had fantasized about it in the past. Did that mean she and she alone was to blame if they broke up for good? She thought it was spectacularly true that it did.

The drive to the airport that morning was as uncomfortable as it was anti-climactic. They embraced before Ray turned and walked into the terminal, neither of them able to speak.

"Krystal, are you sure you're OK?" Strachey's voice startled her, and she realized she had not moved from the chair in front of his desk.

She looked at him, embarrassed. "Yeah, sure, I'm OK."

It was a total lie.

Strachey looked at his watch. "It's afternoon, and I'm hungry. And you look like you could use a drink. Let's finish this over lunch at Fitzgerald's."

She settled into the seat in Strachey's car struggling to clear her mind. "Um, you were saying that I stirred things up in Washington?"

"I think you must have scared old Whitehall out of his britches. The CIA contacted me Saturday morning, but I'm almost certain the orders came from the Hoover Building. They want us to stand down on the Nessmith case."

"What the fuck does that mean?"

"It means, or so my old CIA pal told me, that they think the real target was Gregory Davis, that he and the others were killed by a Russian hit team."

"Like in England?"

"Something like that."

"Well, why don't they say so. It would save us a lot of trouble."

"That's where it gets complicated. The feebies are afraid of more bad publicity if it comes out that the Russians are running around under their noses assassinating defectors in the US."

"Defector? So, Davis was a defector like you thought?"

"So, they told me. His real name was Pushkin, and he worked for one of Putin's dark lords."

"But what about Padruig?"

"Oh, the Feds don't really give a damn. He can be convicted of murder as far as they care, just so long as their little secrets are kept away from the public. And our friend Curry isn't doing us any favors either."

Krystal groaned. "Have I told you how much I hate the CIA?"

"Many times," grinned Strachey as they pulled into parking for the restaurant.

Inside, they took a booth, and Strachey ordered their meals and a couple of beers. She decided a beer wouldn't hurt, and they sipped in silence until their meals arrived, then he asked. "Want to tell me what's wrong now?"

"Not really."

She didn't feel like sharing now, least of all with Robert Strachey whose good-natured *bonhomie* was the polar opposite of how she was feeling. She should have skipped the office and gone straight back to her apartment from the airport. She would not be fit company for human beings today. But she knew if she went home, she would end up drinking alone, and she wanted to avoid falling into that trap again. She looked at the beer. Drinking with someone else was OK, right?

CHAPTER 17

Tuesday morning announced itself with bars of light falling across her face through the blinds in the bedroom window. She awoke with a start and sat straight up in bed, a move she instantly regretted as shards of pain shot through her temples. What time was it? It looked much too bright outside still to be early morning. She raised her wrist to look at her watch and was surprised to see her arm still clad in the sleeve of the blouse she'd worn the day before. She had slept in her clothes. *Well, this isn't looking good,* she thought.

She swayed a bit when she stood to make her way to the bathroom feeling queasy. Her mouth tasted bad and felt like it was stuffed with cotton. She fuzzily recalled driving home, at Strachey's insistence, after yesterday's lunch and digging a bottle of scotch out of the kitchen cupboard. A look in the mirror revealed bleary eyes, smeared make-up, and tangled hair. She must have passed out on the bed. *Christ, I should have been in the office hours ago.*

She brushed her teeth, stripped off the wrinkled clothes and underwear, dropped them in a pile on the floor, and ran the shower until it was steaming before stepping in, letting the hot water pelt her skin before twisting the temperature control to cold and standing under the frigid stream until she felt half-way like a fully functioning human being, or at least a fully awake one. She'd set her watch on the basin and now saw the time was already past ten A.M. She must have slept for nearly twelve hours straight through. She needed fluids badly, or the hangover would be with her the entire day.

She wrapped her hair in a towel and threw on a terrycloth robe, then went to the kitchen where she downed two full water glasses of orange juice accompanied by a couple of aspirin. The headache receded to a dull throb

As she tried to gather her wits, the thought of Ray Velazquez rose like a specter ready to haunt another day. She shoved him back into a dark recess, submerged him beneath the questions at hand regarding the Padruig Nessmith case. She needed desperately to escape the events of yesterday morning, and Nessmith was her lode star.

She needed food, but she knew her stomach would rebel, so she settled for a piece of dry toast that she held between her teeth as she walked to her car.

When she pushed through the doors to PSI Ruth's eyes swept over her from top to bottom before she smiled the way a mother might smile at a sick child. "We weren't sure you would show up today, darlin'. Feelin' OK?"

Krystal grimaced at the greeting. "Yeah, fine. Is Bob in his office?"

Ruth waved vaguely in the direction of Strachey's office. "He's in there," she said breezily, "You can go right in."

It did not improve her mood that Ruth should think she needed permission to see Strachey. They were partners, after all. A sharp retort sprang to her lips, but she repressed it. Maybe she was overreacting. But again, she wondered why Bob had hired Ruth Scatterfield in the first place. She just did not fit in with the modern image Bob said he wanted to project. What they needed was a sharp, efficient younger woman who would surely make a better first impression on clients than the dowdy Ruth. Maybe it was a Southern thing.

She took time to stop at the Keurig and make a cup of extra strong coffee, then pushed open the door, cup in hand, to Strachey's office to find him on the phone. He waved her to a seat, eyebrows raised, as he concluded the call. "... OK, thanks for calling, Tony. No problems from our end."

He replaced the receiver. "That was my old Company friend, Tony DeLorenzo. He wanted to make sure we're keeping our distance from the case."

She was puzzled. "And you agreed? I thought you said we would press on." She couldn't believe he planned to leave Padruig to swing in the wind.

He gave her an appraising look, and ignoring her question asked, "Are you feeling better? I wasn't sure we'd see you today."

She felt the color rising in her cheeks. "Um, yeah, I'm fine. Thanks for the day off."

"A friend in need and all that ..."

She broke in before he could say more. "Let's forget that. What about the CIA?"

"Them? Nothing to worry about. I just want them to stay calm and keep them at a distance."

"So, you lied to them?"

He shot her an evil grin. "Krystal, it is the CIA, after all. They lie to people, and people lie to them all the time. They're used to it. This will keep them off our backs for a while."

"But, won't you get in trouble?"

He snorted and spread his arms wide. "There's nothing they can do to me. I left before I reached retirement age, so they can't threaten my income. I refused to sign their confidentiality agreement, so I'm breaking no laws. They'll be unhappy, but there's really nothing they can do about it."

She wasn't so sure, having seen a lot of movies about the CIA getting even with people who crossed them. "If you say so, Bob, but I don't like it. Every time I've been involved with the Agency things have gotten a little hairy."

"I have an idea," he said.

"I'm all ears.

"I think we can take advantage of the Agency's involvement to advance our investigation."

She liked the idea of taking advantage of the spooks. Turnabout was fair play, after all. "What do you have in mind?"

"Well, DeLorenzo confirmed that Davis aka Pushkin was a defector under their care. It stands to reason that his wife is no stranger to dealing with Agency representatives. I think I should pay her a visit."

"You? But you can't represent yourself as CIA. No matter what you think, that's against the law. You could get into real trouble."

"Ah, my dear, but you underestimate me. I don't plan to tell her I'm with the CIA. But I can drop a hint that I might be."

She still didn't like it. "They'll find out what you're up to right away, and they'll make trouble."

"Maybe. Probably. But it's worth a chance if we find something useful."

"It's still risky."

"Aw, Krystal, you've had most of the fun up 'til now. Give me a chance."

CHAPTER 18

There was no time to spare, so two P.M. that afternoon found Strachey parked a block away from the Pushkin aka Davis house in a rented Lincoln Navigator, black, of course. There were two approaches, and he had chosen the one that brought him down a hill on a winding street to an intersection a short distance from the house. The white Honda Accord with the bike rack described by Krystal was in the carport, and the street in front of the house was empty. There was little traffic in this quiet neighborhood. It being Summer break, there were children playing in some of the yards and a few women were walking dogs. A light rain had fallen earlier, cooling the hot streets and leaving the trees and grass sparkling with drops of water as the sun again claimed hegemony over the sky.

Although only the family car was present Strachey expected the Agency to have posted a watcher with Natasha, maybe someone from the Office of Security. He certainly would have done so, but Agency defector handling practices had never been of particularly high standards. The Brits were probably the best at it among Western services, and he had often advocated emulating them, but as usual the bean counters prevailed. He doubted Natasha was in danger of assassination by Russian agents. Her husband had been the guilty party, and she had been along only for the ride. Having eliminated their prime target, it was unlikely the Russians would lurk around Charlotte waiting for a chance at Natasha. Logic and past practice suggested they would be long gone, perhaps on a plane back to Moscow.

Everything depended on how the watcher, if there was one, reacted to him. He would have either no time or only a limited time to speak with Natasha.

He put the big SUV into gear and rolled down into the street and into the driveway. He'd worn a dark suit, not one of his expensive ones, white shirt, and conservative tie, as well as a pair of non-prescription glasses with thick, black rims. A face appeared at a window as he stepped out of the SUV and walked along the sidewalk to the front door. There was no sound from inside the house. The front entrance was comprised of a combination glass and screened storm door and a wooden door facing a low set of brick steps. He rang the bell.

The door was opened almost immediately, and he recognized Natasha from Krystal's description. "Yes?" she said.

Strachey's Russian was rusty, but he'd practiced a few phrases he hoped would put Natasha at ease. "Mrs. Pushkin," he said with what he hoped was a reassuring smile, "I'm a friend of Mr. DeLorenzo, and I'd like to have a few words with you." It was a calculated risk that she knew DeLorenzo, but the man was from the Russia House, and he was in town.

Natasha Pushkin blinked, confused. "Tony sent you?" she asked.

"He briefed me on your case." Strachey was tiptoeing through a minefield and had to choose his words carefully. "May I come in so we can talk. I won't take much of your time."

"Who is it, Natasha?" a female voice sounded from somewhere in the house.

Michael R. Davidson

Natasha looked back over her shoulder. "It's someone Tony sent to see me."

"Well, let him in," sounded the voice.

Natasha stepped back to allow Strachey to pass and closed the door behind him. They stood in a wide entrance hallway not quite grand enough to be called a foyer. A door to the right led to the kitchen, and to the left another door that evidently led to the bedrooms. Straight ahead, the hallway opened into a living room with a row of windows that provided a view of a surprisingly large and well-kept back yard. A young woman, evidently the source of the voice, appeared at the living room entrance. Strachey put her age at early twenties and guessed she was a relatively recent hire, probably to the Office of Security. Like Natasha, she wore blue jeans and a tank top with sandals on her feet. "Hi, she said. Who are you?"

"I spoke with Tony DeLorenzo a little while ago, and he briefed me on the case. I'd like a short, private conversation with Mrs. Pushkin, if I may."

The girl looked uncertain. Strachey put on his stern face. "What's your name?"

"Erm, Alicia Kensington."

"Well, Alicia, as I said, I need a few quiet words with Mrs. Pushkin here. We'll use the living room. I suggest you find somewhere else comfortable to wait until we're finished."

"But nobody told me ...," began Alicia.

"Do you understand the meaning of 'need to know,' Alicia?" Strachey took unseemly pleasure in using one of the Agency's mantras against it.

"S-sure."

"Excellent. Now make yourself scarce for a little

while. I'll let you know when I'm ready to leave."

Alicia reluctantly retreated into the hallway leading to the bedrooms and closed the door.

Strachey took Natasha gently by the elbow and ushered her into the living room, which was eclectically, but tastefully decorated. An otherworldly yowl startled him, and he spotted an overweight Siamese cat on the sofa, which immediately leapt to the floor and disappeared, tail twitching, in the direction of the kitchen. He led Natasha to the sofa where they both sat down. There was no way to know how much time he would have with her. At this very moment, Alicia could be calling her Agency superiors to report his arrival which could result in the sudden appearance of several large security officers with guns and bad attitudes. He told himself he would refuse to feel embarrassment if this happened.

"Mrs. Pushkin," he began, "did you or your husband notice anything out of the ordinary before the shooting occurred? Strange phone calls? People following you?"

She screwed her face into a frown. "Do you mean, did we see GRU agents hiding behind trees?"

It was impossible to tell whether this was irony or anger. "Something like that, maybe," he said softly, watching her closely.

She relaxed a little and said, "Nothing like that. There was only the phone call."

"Phone call?" DeLorenzo had not mentioned a phone call.

"Yes, but it was not from the Russians. It had nothing to do with the Russians."

"Can you tell me a little more about it?"

She tossed her long, black hair back over one shoulder and looked him straight in the eyes. "But I told Tony all about it."

"I know," he lied. "Will you please tell it again now? It could be important."

She thought for a moment, calling back the memory. "It was a week before Grisha was killed. It was a man from work."

He leaned forward, all his attention concentrated on her. "What man, and what did he say?"

"It was a man from one of the offices Grisha was auditing. Grisha had found some irregularities."

"Did he tell you the name of the man who called?"

"It's a strange name - Raymond Yang." A look of confusion came over her face. "But I told all of this to Tony."

"And what did Tony say?"

"He doesn't think it's important." *DeLorenzo and the FBI were certain Pushkin had been killed by a Russian assassin. Everything else was marginal for therm.*

"Did your husband tell you what Yang said?"

"No. He only laughed and said the man knew he was in big trouble."

"Did Yang threaten your husband?"

A cloud passed over Natasha's face. "I'm not sure. Grisha didn't say."

"So, he didn't think the call was serious?"

"Oh, yes, the trouble was serious, very serious."

"You're sure of this?"

"Oh, yes. It was important enough that Grisha thought he might get a promotion. He was excited and didn't want anyone else to know until he had finished his analysis. He even copied his files onto a thumb drive and brought it home with him to keep them safe."

All of Strachey's antennae were vibrating now. He'd had this feeling in the past when he was on the right track and was almost afraid to ask, "Did you give the thumb drive to Tony?"

She shook her head so her hair fell over one eye and she had to sweep it back with her hand. "Tony didn't seem interested in what Grisha was doing at the bank."

"But you do have the thumb drive?"

"Yes."

"Would you be willing to let me borrow it? I think it could be important."

She frowned, "I'm not sure. The information belongs to the bank."

"I promise it will be closely guarded, and I'll return it immediately. It could be important," he repeated.

This was something she had not anticipated, and she chewed on his words trying to make up her mind. She was, after all, Russian, and that meant she was a natural born skeptic and distrustful of authority. Strachey was familiar with this pattern of behavior. In his Agency days recruiting a Russian was like tempting a timid bird out of the forest with a trail of breadcrumbs.

He was concerned about the amount of time he already had spent in the house. Alicia may have made a phone call or DeLorenzo might show up at any moment. It was past time for him to go.

"Mrs. Pushkin, Natasha, I think this could be important, very important, and I would very much appreciate your cooperation." He quelled his anxiety and hoped his expression was one that would elicit her trust. He felt a pang of conscience at the deception, but only a fleeting one.

Natasha chewed her lower lip. Finally, she said, "All right. I agree if you think it's important." She stood and walked to a small desk that stood against one wall with a laptop resting on it. Strachey followed her. She opened a drawer and withdrew a thumb drive which she handed to him. "This is it."

There was nothing to be gained by staying longer. With luck he would get away clean, although he was certain there would be repercussions.

"Thank you, Natasha. You've been a great help. I'll be in touch."

She walked with him to the front door and stood there watching as he returned to the rented SUV and backed out of the driveway. He saw Alicia come to her side and stare after him as he drove away.

CHAPTER 19

Amy Strachey nee Dawson was beginning to see the advantages of the tranquil Southern life she now enjoyed. She thanked God every day that her father, Thomas Jefferson Dawson, a former Charlotte bus driver, was still with them and seemingly thriving on their return to his native city. Thomas was only too happy to be responsible for looking after their active six-year-old son, Robert Thomas, during the day.

But the tasks she now performed as PSI's cyber chief, she was in fact the ONLY person with those responsibilities, were boring beyond belief. Other than the occasional job designing electronic security systems for customers, there was nothing that came close to challenging her.

She was thinking about what to prepare for dinner that evening when Strachey burst into her office and handed her a thumb drive. "See what you can find on this right away. It might be the break we've been waiting for in the Nessmith case."

She turned the thumb drive over in her hand. "What's supposed to be on it?"

"The records of an audit Grigory Pushkin was working on at the bank. He was worried about security and brought his work home."

"Pushkin was one of the victims in the picnic murders, wasn't he?" Amy had not been involved in the Nessmith case until now.

"That's right."

Merely opening the files on the thumb drive would not exactly be a daunting task. She plugged the stick into her computer and opened it and suddenly things got more interesting. Line after line of meaningless gibberish appeared on her screen.

Strachey, who had been leaning over her shoulder, as much to inhale her perfume as to see the screen, was disappointed. "Crap," he said, "what's all that. Is the information corrupted?"

She knew what she was looking at. "Well," she said, "it looks like Pushkin encrypted some of his files. The ones in the clear seem to be financial records from the H.P.H. Investment Office."

"Can you break them out?"

"Maybe, but it might take some time."

"We don't have a lot of that, and we might have to return the thumb drive."

She smiled. "Not to worry. I'll make a copy. How did you get this?"

"Better you don't know," he said.

"This isn't going to get you into trouble, is it?" Unlike her husband, Amy was not a natural risk taker.

"Well," he drawled, "trouble is a relative concept. Will there BE trouble? Oh, yes, for sure. Will I be in trouble? Maybe a little. I probably pissed off some people, some powerful people. But is there anything they can do about it? I don't think so. But just to be safe, make a copy of that thumb drive right away and give me the original back."

It took her only seconds to accomplish that task. Strachey dropped the thumb drive into his pocket and went out the door whistling Dixie.

*****

His wristwatch told him it was nearing five P.M. which signaled it was past time to break out the scotch and light a cigar. He gave Krystal a ring on the intercom and asked her to join him. The day's skullduggery had put him in a buoyant mood, and he decided it was an appropriate occasion to break the seal on his prized bottle of Lagavulin 25-year-old single malt. The bottle had cost over a thousand dollars, and he had been waiting for an excuse to open it. From his humidor, he selected a cigar that would marry well with such a noble potable, one of his few remaining Cuban Hoyo de Monterey double coronas.

Krystal knocked and entered and gasped when she saw what he was doing. "You're kidding! What's the occasion?"

He grinned like a little boy. "Oh, I'm just feeling good. It was a little like old times today, and I feel like celebrating nostalgia."

"Your spookery, you mean?"

"Damn straight. I enjoyed every minute."

"What happens next?"

"We share some of this nectar." He poured them each a generous measure of the deep, tawny scotch and beheaded his cigar with a silver clipper. He took some time caressing its tip with the flame from a long wooden match before saying more, enjoying her impatience. Satisfied the cigar was properly combusted, he lifted his glass. "To skullduggery," he toasted.

They both sipped carefully and rolled the complex 102 proof liquid over their tongues until the initial dry smoky flavor dissolved into fruity sweetness before swallowing to be rewarded with a spreading and pleasant warmth in their midsections. They looked at one another and smiled.

She knew she should not accept the drink, especially after the disastrous night before. It was illogical. But her body told her otherwise, and there was that old 'hair of the dog' saying. "Holy shit," she said, "I've never tasted anything like that."

"Neither have I." He leaned back in his chair, a sublime smile on his face. The light from the window illuminated the wreath of cigar smoke around his head.

She regarded his bliss with curiosity. "I don't think I've ever seen you so content."

"Ah, it's just the lull before the storm. Let's enjoy it while we can."

She nodded, wondering what he meant, and they sat there quietly enjoying the scotch waiting for the storm to break. They barely had time for another finger of scotch before a commotion in the reception area drew their attention to the door, through which a visibly angry Tony DeLorenzo and a man in a dark suit who could be mistaken for nothing other than a feebie burst in, followed by a white-faced Angela Kensington and an outraged Ruth Scatterfield.

Strachey's grin widened into a smile as DeLorenzo, face red, advanced on his desk. "Hey, Tony," he said, "Nice to see you again."

"You sonuvabitch," gritted DeLorenzo between clenched teeth. "You promised you'd stay out of this, and you're in trouble now, real trouble. It's a Federal offense to impersonate a CIA officer." He gestured behind him at the solemn faced feebie. "This is Special Agent Ron Salinger. I hope he arrests you right now."

Salinger was a tall man with dark hair, a long upper lip, and a solemn air. "Mr. Strachey," he intoned,

"As my colleague from the CIA said, you have committed a federal offense that is punishable by a fine and a jail term. This is very serious. What do you have to say for yourself?"

Krystal stood and took a step to the side of her boss's desk to face the intruders, wondering what would happen now.

Strachey laid a hand on her arm that told her to say or do nothing. He then leaned back in his chair and drew on the fat double corona. He slowly exhaled the luxurious smoke, visibly enjoying it, before speaking. "I didn't commit any offense."

DeLorenzo became even more furious. "Yes, you did, Bob. You pretended to be a CIA officer so you could talk to Natasha Pushkin. After you promised to keep your distance."

"No," Strachey took another leisurely draw on the cigar. "I did no such thing. Ask Alicia here."

DeLorenzo put his hands on the edge of the desk and leaned toward Strachey. "I did ask her. She's the one who reported what you did." He straightened and turned to the young woman. "Tell him, Alicia."

She was obviously frightened. Strachey figured DeLorenzo had threatened her job, and he felt sorry for her, but she probably could find employment more appropriate than the CIA. She was demonstrably unsuited to intelligence work, and he was probably doing her a favor. "H-He came to the door and said he was from the Agency and needed to speak with Natasha. I-I didn't know what to do."

All she needed do, reflected Strachey, was to demand to see his I.D., and the matter would have ended there and then, but she was too green and too easily intimidated. As he recalled, she hadn't even demanded to know his name. DeLorenzo must have recognized him from her physical description.

Strachey's voice overrode her. "Now, Alicia, think back. Did I ever once say I was from the Agency?"

"Y-you said Mr. DeLorenzo sent you."

"Now, now, Alicia. That's not right. I said DeLorenzo had briefed me on the Pushkin matter. I never once said I was from the Agency or any other Federal outfit, now did I?"

Alicia was thoroughly confused. "I-I'm not sure. But I thought you were from the Agency."

"Never mind that now," interjected DeLorenzo. "Natasha gave you something, and we want it back."

Strachey reached into his pocket and withdrew the thumb drive. "You mean this?" He held it out, and DeLorenzo snatched it from his hand.

"So," continued Strachey, "let's clear this up right now. I never said I represented any agency of the Federal Government or any other government for that matter. I spoke nothing but the truth - that Tony here had briefed me, which he did, and I wanted to speak with Natasha Pushkin. No one asked to see any credentials."

"I don't believe you," said DeLorenzo, his black stubbled chin sticking out. He shot an evil look at Alicia.

"Well, Tony," said Strachey, "that's too bad, but I really don't care what you do or don't believe. What's more, I recorded the entire visit to the Pushkin house so there could be no mistaking what I had said or how I represented myself." He had not actually done this though he now wished he had.

DeLorenzo looked helplessly at the feebie who was studying Alicia. "Think hard, Alicia," he said, "is Mr. Strachey correct? Did he say he was from the Agency or did he not?"

Alicia looked to DeLorenzo for help, but the feebie stopped her. "Just tell us the truth about what happened. Is what Mr. Strachey says correct?"

She concentrated for a moment, searching for a clear memory. "I just don't remember," she blurted at last. "He got me all confused."

Strachey thought the feebie might be enjoying DeLorenzo's discomfiture. "Well," he said, "in the absence of solid evidence, I don't think we can go any further with this. But I warn you, Mr. Strachey, if you interfere in our business again, in any way, I repeat, in any way, there will be consequences of a sort you will not like. There could be a review of your license to operate here in Charlotte, your credentials could be questioned, your taxes might be audited. There are a lot of things that could happen if there is a repeat of today's performance. As it is, you are teetering on the line between legality and illegality. I strongly suggest that you take a step back."

DeLorenzo's lips twisted into a nasty smile.

Strachey returned the feebie's stare. "I understand, Special Agent Salinger. I can assure you we have no more interest in your investigation or Russian illegals. But I feel badly to have put you to so much trouble. Would you folks care for a drink? I have some Johnny Walker in the bar."

He wasn't about to offer them a taste of the Lagavulin. Krystal quickly covered her mouth to conceal a smirk.

Salinger's eyes scanned the bottle of Lagavulin. "I think we'll be going, thank you," he said, and the three visitors trooped out the door.

As soon as they were gone, Ruth, who had waited nervously just outside the door, rushed in. "What in the world was that about?" she asked. Then she caught sight of the one-thousand-dollar bottle of scotch. "You opened it!" she exclaimed.

"And we were just about to call you when that gang broke in," said Strachey. In fact, he had been so full of himself that he had forgotten about Ruth.

CHAPTER 20

Ruth was not a scotch drinker, but she enjoyed the conviviality of Happy Hour in the office, and she was delighted to work with Strachey. She refused his offer of the Lagavulin and settled for a glass of *fino* Sherry instead, which she quaffed quickly without sitting down. "I've got to go," she said. "Edward is waiting for his walk." Edward was her dog, a fat pug that she doted over and occasionally brought to the office where he lay at her feet dozing and snoring loudly all day long. Krystal thought the flat-faced creature was the ugliest and laziest animal she'd ever seen. Her family had always had a dog back on the farm, but it had been a working dog, not a weird Chinese experiment in genetic engineering.

Strachey poured them more scotch, a more generous pour this time, which left the level in the bottle at about half. In the back of Krystal's mind an alarm bell was clanging, but her body's hunger had been switched on by the first taste which had warmed her throughout and calmed the tempest in her mind. A little more wouldn't hurt.

Strachey's cigar had developed a long ash which dropped onto his desktop and disintegrated into a messy pile on the shiny surface which he surveyed with the look of a three-year-old who had just spilled his milk. Krystal snorted, expelling some scotch through her nose. Recovering her dignity, she asked, "Why did you hire that woman? Wouldn't we be better off with some young, pretty thing at reception?"

Strachey took a slightly imprecise swipe at the

pile of ashes, leaving a long, gray smudge on the desk. He looked up, surprised by the question. "Ruth? She's a treasure. There's no reason you should know about her, of course. Back in the day she was married to a guy who was a Chief of Station in Eastern Europe. He dropped dead of a heart attack, and Ruth came back to work at Langley. She's smart, competent, and efficient, and she knows how to keep her mouth shut when required. I knew she'd retired here in town and looked her up. Believe me, we're lucky to have her. You just haven't learned to appreciate her yet. You'll see." He poured them another drink and lifted his glass. "To old friends," he toasted.

She found something inexpressibly sad in those words and was horrified to feel a large, oily tear roll down her cheek. She tried to wipe it away before he had seen it but failed.

Her throat momentarily refused to make the sounds required for speech, so she downed the rest of her scotch to cover her embarrassment and held out the empty glass for a refill. She decided she wouldn't mind getting wasted again.

Strachey's face was expressionless as he poured them each another measure. The former spook was not as adept at hiding his thoughts as he believed. Whether it was the whisky loosening her inhibitions or the fact that Robert Strachey was one of the few people she felt she could trust, she blurted, "It's that fucking Cuban, Bob. I'm not sure if it's only one of us or both to blame, but I think it's over."

Now that she'd broached the subject, Strachey clearly wished she hadn't. "I don't know what to say, Krystal, but I'm willing to listen."

So submerged in her own thoughts that she didn't hear what he said, the details of the disastrous weekend spilled out. "And why should he put it all on me?" she asked. "He could move, too. I like Miami, but it's not a place I want to live. But maybe it's not really about that. Maybe I'm just not made for a permanent relationship. Maybe it's impossible for me. We'd probably end up hating one another, and it all would be wasted anyway. There must be something wrong with me - wrong inside, in my head."

Finding herself in such a fragile and uncertain state was unnerving. Her normal reaction to adversity was to challenge it. This was self-flagellation, and she didn't like it because it could eat at her until it consumed her entirely.

Strachey tried to sound convincing. "Krystal," he said, "there's nothing wrong with you. Everyone hits a rough patch now and then."

The words were banal, the sort of thing your mother might say to you if you skinned your knee, and from the look on his face, Strachey realized it. He was feeling the strong whisky now, too, and in lieu of saying more, he poured them each another dollop.

Reinforced by the scotch, he began, "Krystal, that was lame. Now, listen to me. There's absolutely nothing wrong with you. You're smart, brave, and absolutely lovely." His face reddened under his tan, and he finished lamely. "Any man would be lucky to be with you, and only an idiot would pass up the chance."

Fortunately, before he said something he would truly regret, Amy poked her head through the door to announce she had broken Pushkin's code.

They had been rather sadly contemplating the

nearly empty bottle. Strachey was leaning forward, his tie loosened, and looked embarrassed and vaguely guilty. Krystal was gripping the arms of her chair as though she feared she might fall out of it.

"Oh, my God," said Amy, eying the bottle, "You two drank an entire bottle?"

Both stared at her uncomprehendingly, apparently having a little trouble focusing, and assumed quasi serious miens. "It was not just any bottle," said Strachey defensively. It was L-lavalugin, er Lagavulin 25-year old shingle malt. An' it was worth every penny of the thousand bucks I spent on it."

Krystal nodded her head perhaps a bit too enthusiastically. She suddenly felt dizzy and didn't dare try to speak.

CHAPTER 21

Krystal opened her eyes and rubbed the sleep from them with the back of her hand. She was disoriented until she recognized the outlines of her own apartment in the dim light coming through the curtains. Someone had closed them. She was lying on her living room sofa, fully dressed except for her shoes. She started to sit up but was immediately engulfed in a wave of nausea, and a shard of pain shot through her eye and out the back her head. Her mouth was dry. She lay there, one arm over her face, gathering the strength to attempt to sit up again. She tried to focus on a single object to make the room stop spinning. Another quarter hour passed before she thought she could stand. She was desperate for a glass of cold water, and the kitchen was tantalizingly close.

She got unsteadily to her feet, and the room started spinning again, nearly causing her to fall, but she regained her balance and staggered into the kitchen feeling her gorge rise. She made it to the sink before she vomited a pale slightly green, bitter liquid. She stood there, both hands on the sides of the sink for support, ran some cold water and splashed her face, and then filled a glass from the tap and gulped it down.

She had no memory of how she had gotten home. She drank another glass of water and forced down a third to combat the dehydration. The nausea receding a fraction, she made her way to the bathroom and rummaged through the medicine cabinet until she found a bottle of aspirin and swallowed two.

She shed her rumpled clothing on the bedroom

floor and ran the shower. She stood under the steaming water for a long time.

What time is it? The living room curtains had been drawn, but sunlight was pouring through the kitchen window. Belatedly, she checked her watch which fortunately was waterproof because she'd worn it into the shower. It was nearly 11:00 AM.

She wrapped herself in a robe and returned to the kitchen where she brewed a cup of strong coffee in her Keurig. She needed something solid in her stomach but was certain she could keep nothing down. She brewed another cup of coffee and sat at the kitchen table until she could think beyond her physical condition. The previous day came back in bits and pieces, and she was jolted by the fuzzy recollection of telling Strachey about her problem with Ray Velazquez. She'd blabbed the whole sad and embarrassing tale to him like some lovesick schoolgirl. *He must think I'm a total jerk.* How could she face him again? *That damned scotch.*

She was horrified to think Strachey had brought her home and laid her on the sofa, but then hazily recalled Amy with her arm supporting her leading to the elevator and the apartment. Amy. If there was anyone she should have spilled her guts to, it was sweet, gentle Amy and not her husband. Strachey was her boss, and certain rules of conduct applied, even if they were friends.

A great big bubble of anxiety was filling her chest, and she nearly screamed to release the pressure. With relief she remembered it was Saturday, so she would not have to go into the office. She resolved not to step outside the apartment today or maybe ever.

The phone rang, and she trudged back to the living room. The caller I.D. told her it was Amy. She almost didn't answer, but that would be churlish, so she lifted the receiver. "Amy?"

"Yes. I'm just calling to check on you. Are you OK? Do you need anything?" Amy's voice was full of concern, and Krystal wondered how much Strachey had told her about their conversation.

"I'm OK," she said, "but a little hung over, which should be no surprise to you. Thanks for getting me home. I'm so sorry and ashamed."

"We all have those days, Krystal, and I gave Bob a dressing down for opening that bottle at the office. If you need to talk about anything you know I'm here for you." *Of course, Strachey told her everything.*

"Thanks, Amy, but I think I've said enough already. I'll be all right."

"Well, you know where I am. You're important to us, dear, and a friend. It's what friends are for. It's a standing offer."

"Yeah, well, thanks again, Amy. Er, how's Bob?" *Anything to change the subject.*

Amy laughed. "Oh, he's still asleep, or unconscious might be a better term. I can't wait for him to wake up. I'll make his life miserable."

"He'll be miserable without any help, judging from the way I feel."

Amy laughed again. "He's supposed to drive us all up to Asheville for lunch today. A promise is a promise."

"Maybe you should do the driving, especially if he feels the way I do. I don't plan to leave the apartment for a couple of days. I think I'll just go to bed and sleep it off." She wondered if the trip to Asheville might also serve for Strachey to have a look at the home for girls Gavenia had told her about. Strachey liked to mix work with play.

"We'll see," said Amy. "You take good care of yourself, and don't hesitate to call if you need anything."

Krystal replaced the receiver. Her hair was still damp, so she returned to the bathroom and stood in front of the mirror with the blow dryer, staring into her own eyes as she combed out her hair. She never wore much make-up and decided to go without it entirely today, not wanting to take the time to put it on. She picked out jeans and an American University T-shirt, slipped on some flip-flops and returned to the living room.

It was nearing noon. Maybe it was not such a good idea to sit alone and brood. The break-up with Ray plagued her, filling her with indecision that made it impossible for her to leave it behind. Alcohol had certainly not helped, exposing personal pain she would have preferred to keep hidden. She would get over it eventually, she believed, but last evening had ripped the scab from her wound and set her back.

Ray had freed her from the creeping loneliness of spinsterhood and checked a box on the normalcy side of the ledger. She was not the unpredictable lone wolf, unapproachable and cold. She was as capable of a romantic relationship as any woman. But in the end had she taken Ray for granted? Was it fair to think he would always be there, waiting for her without complaint? She knew it wasn't, but what did that say about her? Was she so selfish, so self-absorbed, so needful to be in command that she was incapable of committing to a relationship and everything that entailed? No. That was a comfortable illusion. The world did not revolve around her. Ray had every right to expect more.

And if this were so, what were her true feelings about him? Was he nothing more than a convenience, an outlet for her sexual needs to be at her beck and call? Ray was a normal human being, and more, a real man with needs and expectations of his own to which he had every right.

The break-up was entirely her fault, and its inevitability should have been evident from the beginning if she had been honest with herself. She would have to learn how to live with that or change. And if she could not change the implications for her future frightened her.

CHAPTER 22

Monday morning, they gathered again in Strachey's office. Amy noticed that Strachey and Krystal avoided looking at one another. She assumed this initial mutual embarrassment would pass as the day progressed. Her husband had not fulfilled his promise to drive the family to Asheville on Saturday, which had put Thomas Jefferson Dawson in a peculiar mood that vacillated between disappointment and hilarity.

She had important information to share with the group which should set something in motion - she wasn't sure what. "If you recall," she used the phrase with delicious mischievousness, drilling her husband with a look, "I told you on Friday that I broke Pushkin's encryption system. What I uncovered was a pile of bank documents that will require some analysis if we are to understand them. This might take some time as I'm not an accountant. And there's another problem. These documents belong to the bank. They're all marked confidential. Is it legal for us to keep them?"

The bank doesn't know we have them," said Strachey, "and what they don't know won't hurt them."

Amy wasn't so sure. "It might hurt if it shows something significant about bank operations, or it could come back to bite us you know where."

Strachey rubbed his chin. "I dunno," he said. "It depends."

"Depends on what?" asked Amy.

"Well," said Strachey, "we didn't acquire the documents from the bank. We got them from Pushkin's thumb drive. The way I see it, it's just like a reporter getting an inside tip, like the Pentagon Papers. The guy who leaked could be prosecuted, but the newspaper gets off Scot free. Pushkin's dead, so they can't do anything to him."

Amy chewed on this for a few beats. "OK, yeah, but what about Julian Assange?"

"Assange acted as a spy. He didn't behave like a journalist."

"Well," replied Amy, "We don't even know what the documents mean yet. It could be a lot of nothing."

"Or," interjected Krystal, "it could be what got Pushkin killed."

"The documents are mostly spreadsheets and financial statements," said Amy. "We need to find someone who can make sense of them."

"Maybe we already have someone," said Strachey. He punched a button on the intercom and asked Ruth to join them. Turning to Amy and Krystal, he said, "Ruth spent years handling Division finances and more. They even sent her to a course on finance, and she ended up getting her degree. It's a long shot, but it's worth a try. I wouldn't like to have to look for an accountant outside the office, especially on this case."

When she was filled in, Ruth was enthusiastic. "Well, my goodness," she drawled, "it's about time I had somethin' really interestin' to do around here. I'm not just a pretty face, you know."

"But a very pretty face you are, Ruth," said Strachey with a broad smile, the first time he'd looked relaxed since Friday night.

Krystal still had doubts about Ruth, but she kept

them to herself. *Who knows? The damned spooks are always full of surprises.* It seemed odd to think that this plump, middle-aged lady who favored pastels as a fashion choice and spoke like everyone's idea of a southern belle, if a somewhat fading one, had spent a lifetime in the murky world of espionage. It was something Krystal could never have endured because she abhorred ambiguity, and obscurantism was the prime rule of the spooks. The world for Krystal was dichotomous, black and white, right or wrong, and she was certain that spies somewhere along the line lost the ability to distinguish between the two.

"What do you think we should be doing while Ruth goes over the documents," she asked.

Strachey scratched his chin, then said, "We should check out this Raymond Yang fellow. We know nothing about him except that he works at H.P.H. Bank. Where does he live? Is he living beyond his means? How long has he been with H.P.H. and what are his responsibilities there?" He turned to Amy. "Sweetie, can you run a check on him? We need a picture, from driver's license records if all else fails, and we need an address. And see if you can get into the bank's database, see if there's something there we can use."

Amy frowned. "The bank won't be easy, and it's not quite kosher, but I think I can do it."

He replied, "As long as you don't get caught."

"Oh," she said, "I won't get caught. I'll route the inquiry through all sorts of servers. Even if they detect the hack, which they shouldn't even discover, they won't be able to trace it to us."

"That's my girl."

Krystal remained silent, but she was thinking,

What the hell are we doing? It's as though breaking the law simply doesn't matter. They were using stolen bank documents, and now they planned to hack into a private server. Everything she had stood for as a police officer screamed at her that this was wrong, but Strachey and Amy didn't bat an eye at the idea of illegality so long as it got them what they wanted. And what was worse, she was part of it. She was a lawbreaker. In her experience, once someone stepped over that line, there was no going back, and it led to even greater violations and the risks they entailed.

And this led her back to exactly what she wanted to avoid - thoughts of Ray Velazquez and the life they might have made together in Miami. She could still be a police officer doing what she had trained and worked so hard to be.

But what could she do? Report what they were doing to Captain Curry? No. It would be unthinkable to betray her friends. There was no choice at this point but to go with the flow and hope for the best.

Strachey had known her long enough to read the indecision in her face. "Krystal, you seem concerned about something. Remember, what we are doing here is all in-house. Nothing will escape these walls. You're concerned about the way we're going about things, but we're not the police. We're not lawyers. We're an investigative agency, and we work with all the tools at our disposal. Yes, occasionally we cut some legal corners, and there is a slight risk, but we're very good at what we do, and we do nothing without careful consideration.

Krystal's lips formed a wry smile. "Nobody ever thinks they'll be caught," she said.

No one said a word until Amy spoke up in a quiet voice. "You know, the guy might have a Facebook or Twitter account. Who doesn't these days? We may have been getting ahead of ourselves. And don't you think we should find out what's in the bank documents we have already before we try breaking into the bank's records? I'll try open sources first. Krystal is right to be cautious. We're not with the Government any longer."

Strachey's brow furrowed in what Krystal suspected was momentary chagrin, but then he nodded and said, "OK. Try it that way. But if it doesn't work, we'll have to re-think it." Turning to Krystal, he asked with a trace of sarcasm, "All better now?"

She returned his stare coldly. "Maybe 'we'll have to re-think it,'" she mimicked Strachey's voice and immediately regretted it because it sounded petty and rash. She turned abruptly on her heel and strode out of the office leaving three open mouths in her wake.

CHAPTER 23

Krystal closed her office door and leaned against the frame with her eyes closed. Strachey's sarcastic comment echoed in her ears. She sat heavily at her desk and put her face in her hands. *What's the matter with me? It's the same everywhere.* No matter what she did or where she worked, she somehow always managed to question procedural orders and alienate superiors.

It had to be more than just what her mother called her "Irish." She was convinced it was some sort of deep-seated character flaw she found impossible to overcome. She had been fortunate in the past to survive her *contretemps,* even to triumph, but that was of little comfort now. She may have alienated her friend.

A soft knock at her office door intruded on her self-recriminations. Normally, it was agreed that a closed door meant no interruption, and she was surprised. There was another knock, more insistent this time. She quickly composed her face. "Come in," she said, holding her voice steady.

Robert Strachey stood for a moment at the threshold studying her before he stepped inside and closed the door behind him. He took a seat in front of her desk before speaking, his voice strained with repressed emotion. "Krystal, I know you're upset, and I've come to apologize to you. You were right to be concerned about where we were heading with the investigation, and I want you to know that I ... we all appreciate it. In fact, it's one of the reasons we feel so good about having you with us. I did tell you to be up front with me, after all. You have experience we do not, and we need you to hold us back when it looks like we might be going over a cliff. Every office needs a conscience, and we're very fortunate to have you."

Her throat constricted, and she was unable to speak for a few beats. "Thanks, Bob," she began, "I'm sorry. Things have been a little crazy lately." Her voice faltered.

"You have no reason to apologize," he said. "Amy and I understand, and we're here for you. You know that, I hope."

All she could do was nod and choke out, "Thanks." She couldn't meet his eyes, embarrassed by her uncharacteristic emotionalism.

Strachey left, closing the door softly behind him.

She sat unmoving for a long time letting the silence seep in and fill her until calmness returned. *"We're here for you"* Strachey had said and meant it. Her normal practice when feeling stress was to isolate it, drop it into a dark pit until it fell so far that it could be forgotten. This time, she had been unable to do so. Instead, she had sought relief in a bottle.

Maybe she was not so alone, after all, though the space once occupied by Velazquez remained a painful hollow in her chest. If she continued along this path, she would end up a lonely and bitter person, like Padruig Nessmith, almost entirely unwilling or incapable of relating to other people. She could not allow that to happen. *Lord, I'm becoming maudlin. I'm doing this to myself. It's got to stop.*

The preceding week had taken its toll and led to today's blow-up in Strachey's office. She resolved not to let it happen again.

CHAPTER 24

By Wednesday Amy had collected enough data on Wang to call a meeting. Ruth had been working on Pushkin's documents for the past two days. At ten A.M. they gathered around the mahogany table in the conference room. Ruth made coffee for everyone and a cup of tea for herself.

"There is no lack of information from open sources on Yang," announced Amy. "There's a photo and short biography on the bank's webpage where he's listed as an Executive Vice President, and his wife is active on Facebook. According to the phone book and a check on Google Earth, he has a nice house out in Elizabeth. He was born in California." She turned to Krystal who was still not completely familiar with Charlotte geography. "Elizabeth is a suburb a little east of town. His Facebook account shows he's married with two kids." She passed around a photo she had downloaded from the Internet. It showed a young-looking man of Chinese descent in a business suit giving a closed mouth smile to the camera.

Strachey's interest was piqued. "He's an Executive Vice President? That must be pretty high up in the bank's food chain."

Amy nodded. "He's probably making two hundred K a year plus benefits."

Strachey gave a low whistle. "So, we have a bank muckety-muck like this phoning a relatively low-level employee who's been with the bank only a year and making threats. That's interesting, especially when you put it together with Pushkin transferring data to a thumb drive and taking it home. What was Pushkin up to?"

"Depending on what's on the thumb drive, maybe he was thinking of blackmailing Yang," said Amy with a glance at Ruth.

"Could be," said Strachey, "That would be a strong motive for murder. But DeLorenzo described Pushkin as a very honest guy. His disgust at corruption was the reason he defected. Blackmail would be out of character."

"And would someone in his situation take the risk of breaking the law after so short a time in the country?" asked Krystal. "I think it's more likely he wanted to protect the information."

"Uh-huh," said Strachey. "Whatever is on the thumb drive meant 'serious trouble' for Yang, according to Natasha. Maybe trouble so serious it could be a motive for murder."

"So," asked Krystal, "you think the CIA and the feebies are chasing a wild goose?"

"That's another question entirely," said Strachey. "They're deadly serious about Russian illegals and claim they have some corroborative information. Running a dragnet over the entire Southeast is a big, expensive deal, probably involving hundreds of FBI agents. So, we can't discount the possibility that they're onto something real."

"I might have something." They had nearly forgotten that Ruth Scatterfield was sitting at the table with them and were startled when she spoke up. All of them turned curious eyes toward her, while she took a dainty sip of tea.

"What's that, Ruth?" asked Strachey.

"Well," she pronounced it 'way-ul' with a sweet Carolina lilt. "I've been going through the documents from the thumb drive. Mr. Yang is the chief trader in the bank's Investment Office. I looked up what such offices do, and it seems they are responsible for limitin' the bank's risk through investments, sort of like a hedge fund. It's a way to protect the bank from unexpected losses as well as add to the bottom line."

"You mean the bank invests in the stock market?" asked Krystal.

"In a way," replied Ruth. "Mostly they play it high and wide in the derivatives market. And that can be dangerous, of course."

"How so?" asked Krystal. She had no idea how derivatives worked.

"Way-ul, y'all remember 2008 when the bottom dropped out of housing prices?" Everyone nodded. "Some derivatives are based on mortgage-backed securities. If the value drops, you can lose a whole lot of money. You see, they can 'own' these securities by only puttin' in 10 or 15 percent of the cash value. But if the value of the security drops instead of goin' up, they have to keep puttin' more money in to cover the difference. The first time property values dropped like that was the Great Depression. Trouble with this kind of financial instrument is that no one really knows what they're worth so valuations can be wild."

"That's gobbledygook to me," said Krystal.

"But that's the way it is, darlin'" smiled Ruth. "Remember, in 2008 the whole economy dropped into a recession because the banks overreached in mortgage backed securities."

"How does this relate to Pushkin's files?" asked

Strachey, impatient for her to get to the point.

"I'm still studyin' it," said Ruth. "These files are dense, but I can tell you this, the bank was losin' ground to margin calls in futures trades when the price of oil fell. And it looks like there was a bunch of other bad investments, as well. But there were others that showed a profit. It sort of evens out."

"I don't see how that could be a motive for murder," grumbled Strachey.

Ruth favored them with an arch smile, having saved the best for last. "It could be, if they were hidin' gains as losses," she said. "But the real kicker is that there's another set of records with almost the same data with one exception. And you know what they're doin'? They're hidin' the gains, at least some of them, in dribs and drabs."

Everyone stared at her for a moment. Finally, Strachey spoke up. "You mean to say that Pushkin somehow managed to get his hands on two different sets of books for the same accounts?"

Ruth nodded. "Somehow, the trader, presumably Mr. Yang, had to keep track of what was really happening. If he didn't, things could easily fly out of control. And they don't use paper ledgers anymore. He must have hidden the file somewhere in the database he thought was safe and protected it with a password. That Russian fella must have been pretty smart to have sussed it all out the way he did."

"You said there was only one difference between the records?" asked Strachey.

Ruth nodded. "Way-ul, not exactly. You see, your dead Russian discovered that wherever there was a profit, the amounts are slightly lower on one ledger than the other. He added all the discrepancies which go back several years and found the exact same amounts as the discrepancies were regularly deposited into the account of a bank customer called Emerald Trading Partners. The account is in the Cayman Islands. Now, this company, Emerald Trading Partners, appears in both data sets, but in one they invest small amounts with the bank, and in the other they receive much larger cash transfers."

Krystal's heart was beating a little faster now. "Well," she breathed, "that sounds like a motive for murder to me. They're skimming money that belongs to the bank into their own account." She discovered a newfound respect for Ruth.

"I agree," said Strachey with an enthusiasm that betrayed his own excitement. "Well done, Ruth, very well done. How much money are we talking about?"

Ruth beamed at them and took another sip of tea. "Way-ul, accordin' to the records this has been goin' on for some time, like I said. The total deposits add up to over a hundred million dollars, almost a piddlin' amount for the bank, but high on the hog for individuals."

Strachey whistled. "The question is," he said, turning to Krystal, "do we take this information to the police or do we continue investigating on our own?"

He was looking directly at Krystal, and she knew why. "The police are heavily invested in Padruig Nessmith, and the feebies think it was some sort of Russian assassination and want the cops to hold onto Padruig for cover. I can't see any of them buying into a new theory until we have a lot more information."

"There's something else," said Amy. "We need to

find out who owns Emerald Trading Partners. For my money, no pun intended, that information is crucial."

"Dollars to donuts," said Krystal, "the account belongs to Raymond Yang."

Amy agreed. "That seems the most likely, but it's still just speculation. Obviously, Yang is in the scam up to his neck, but he may not be alone or even the chief culprit. But it's tricky trying to peek into bank files in the Cayman Islands, maybe impossible. I could have done it, maybe, back at the Agency with the right tools from NSA, but here?"

Strachey considered this and said. "OK, then, the next step is to mount a surveillance against Yang."

*****

Krystal volunteered for the first shift of the surveillance of Raymond Yang, which began early the next morning. It gave her an excuse to go to bed early and avoid drinking because she had to be fresh.

She rented a nondescript mid-sized car at an agency on South Boulevard and was parked down the street from Yang's house at seven A.M. Thursday, after stopping at a MacDonald's for a breakfast sandwich and a surprisingly good cup of coffee. She'd have to watch the coffee intake because peeing behind bushes was frowned upon in Charlotte, but she was incapable of starting the day without it.

The house was a McMansion that filled most of a quarter-acre lot. In this neighborhood Krystal estimated the house would have cost well over a half-million dollars. The driveways were occupied by a variety of BMW's, Mercedes, and Audis, with the occasional top of the line American make.

The day promised more Summer heat, and Krystal hoped her target would begin moving soon. She didn't want to leave the engine running, but in a few hours air conditioning would be *de rigeur*.

She regretfully placed the empty paper cup in the McDonalds bag with the detritus of her breakfast and reclined the seat back until she was looking through the steering wheel. Surveillance operations involve a lot of waiting interspersed with short bursts of activity. She expected to see nothing unusual. Yang would most likely drive to the bank where he would remain most of the day. It would be more interesting to see what he did after work and on weekends. Of course, there was no guarantee the surveillance would reveal anything, at all.

At 7:30 Yang's garage door opened, and a moment later a late model Mercedes E-Class sedan backed into the street and pulled away. Wishing she had more coffee, she raised her seat back to the driving position and followed at a discreet distance. As expected, Yang drove directly to the bank, and his car disappeared into the attached multi-level parking garage. The only new information Krystal gleaned was that Yang was an appallingly poor driver.

She parked across the street from the bank and sat there pondering her next move. She didn't intend to sit there all day as it was unlikely Wang would leave before the bank's closing time. What she was considering was whether she could get into the parking garage and examine the Mercedes.

She watched the entrance for a while. There was no guard. Entry was controlled by a barrier that lifted when a card was inserted into a card reader. After half an hour, she had seen many employees enter the garage. She assumed there was an interior entrance to the bank.

By 9:30 the flow of employees had petered out, and she decided to see if she could find Yang's car. Strachey would probably think it was too early to take chances, but she was bored. She crossed the street and walked up the ramp where she paused at the entrance, watching and listening for signs that someone was inside. Hearing nothing, she proceeded into the dark interior, stopping just inside past the barrier.

The garage consisted of three decks, each with a door on the interior wall that presumably led to a staircase. Given the security screening she'd passed through when she met Pushkin's boss, she could assume there was a security post or card reader behind each door. She was wearing jeans, sneakers, and a black T-shirt and had taken the precaution of donning dark glasses and stuffing her hair under a baseball cap. She was right to have done so because she spotted cctv cameras mounted high up on the walls. From what she had seen, the bank's security was tight, so she turned on her heel and walked slowly back down the ramp and across the street wondering if there was an exterior camera following her. It was much too early in the game to risk unwelcome questions from bank security. There would be other opportunities. She got in the car and drove away.

CHAPTER 25

After two days, surveillance had uncovered nothing suspicious about Yang. It was Friday just after noon, and Krystal was in the office. One of her newly hired contract men would cover the bank at closing time. They hoped Friday evening would bring Yang out, but they weren't hopeful that it would reveal anything.

Her desk phone rang. The line was routed through the front desk, so Ruth answered whenever there was a call. "It's Sergeant Wolf from the police," she announced in Krystal's ear. "Should I put him through?"

Krystal said, "Sure. I'll talk to him."

Given the tone of their last meeting with Captain Curry she was both surprised and intrigued that his Chief of Staff wanted to talk to her.

The phone clicked as Ruth transferred the call. "Sergeant Wolf," said Krystal in what she hoped was a welcoming tone, "what can I do for you?"

The Sergeant's voice had a backwoods twang that reminded her of Frank Watson back in Arlington. She couldn't recall his having spoken at all during their first meeting with Curry, but she remembered piercing blue eyes that bespoke a sharp intelligence. "I need to have a conversation with you," he said, "but not over the phone. Is there someplace we can meet?"

Curiouser and curiouser. "Hey, it's your town, Sergeant, you say where and when."

Wolf's response was not immediate, and she could picture him thinking. Finally, he said, "Scene of the crime. Six o'clock. I'll meet you in the parking lot."

As soon as she hung up, she dashed to Strachey's office. "You'll never guess who just called," she breathlessly announced.

She told him about Wolf's call which elicited a low whistle from him. "Maybe he has a message from Curry. More threats to get us off the case."

"That's logical," she said, "but why act so secretive about it, and why call me instead of you. If Curry was involved, they could always call us back to their office, not set up a semi-clandestine meeting. I think it's something else."

"Well, we'll find out this evening. In the meantime, I think it's prudent to pause the surveillance on Wang."

"You think he's noticed and called the cops?"

"I doubt he could have spotted us, but you never know. Let's find out what the cops want and then decide how to proceed."

*****

Krystal arrived early at the rendezvous. The park was far from empty as the longer days of summer kept people there later into the evening. She pulled into an empty space in the parking lot and settled down to wait. She'd rushed home after informing Strachey and changed into jeans, her Arlington County Police T-shirt, and sneakers. More out of habit than anticipation of trouble, her Smith & Wesson .380 was tucked inside her jeans in a soft inside-the-belt holster.

At precisely six o'clock a late model black Jeep Wrangler with oversized knobby tires drew up in the space beside her. Its sides were liberally spattered with mud. From behind the wheel, Sergeant Archie Wolf stared at her for a second before getting out and walking to the side of her VW. She opened the passenger side window and he leaned in. "Let's get out and walk," he said in his twangy voice. He was not in uniform either and was now clad in similar style to Krystal: jeans, a white polo shirt worn outside his pants, and black half-boots. The short sleeves revealed stringy, muscular arms. In the sunlight his narrow face and sharp features reminded her more of a ferret than a wolf.

She stood out of her car and scanned the lot, which elicited a reaction from Wolf. "I'm here alone," he said in a pleasant baritone voice. "And," he added with a smirk, "I'm a police officer. You're perfectly safe."

Only slightly embarrassed, she walked around the car. Wolf held out his hand, and she took it. His handshake was firm and dry. "Thanks for coming," he said. "I wasn't sure you would."

"You said you had something to tell me," she said. She leaned back against her car and folded her arms, waiting for him to speak.

"I said we needed to have a conversation." His ice blue eyes didn't leave her face which at a subliminal level pleased her because most men's eyes inevitably strayed down to her chest as though drawn there by some primeval force.

"OK, so let's talk. What's this about?"

"Let's walk," he said, waving vaguely in the direction of the park.

She pushed off the car and followed him in silence, her curiosity building, until they were on the footpath which led around the pond where the murders took place. He said, "I don't like what's happening with

Padruig Nessmith, and I'm certain you know as well as I that he had nothing to do with the murders."

She hadn't expected this and wasn't sure how to respond.

"Does your boss agree?" she asked.

Wolf shrugged his narrow shoulders. "Curry has some political irons in the fire. He likes the publicity, but I'm not sure he sees your client as a killer. The Feds have him boxed in, though, and even if he wanted, which he doesn't, there's nothing he can do."

"Does Curry know you're talking to me?"

Wolf barked a sharp laugh, like an axe splitting wood. "Hell no," he said. "He'll skin me if he finds out. I'd be back walking a beat with fewer stripes on my sleeve."

Krystal wasn't sure she believed him, but she wanted to. He was beginning to sound like an earlier version of herself in the Arlington County Police. "So," she asked, "why are you here?"

"I'd like to know where you and your boss are in the investigation."

Aha! "First, he's my partner, not my boss," she began, "And second, why should I trust you with any information. You're likely just to take it straight to Curry, who is your boss."

One corner of his mouth twitched upward as he stopped walking and turned to face her. She returned his stare.

"I can see how you would think that," he said, "but it's the last thing I'd do, for the time being anyhow. How about this: let's start over again, cop to cop. Let me tell you what I think and see where we go from there."

His denial was beginning to ring true, and the reason he had called her rather than Strachey was that she had been a cop. "Sounds OK to me. Shoot." She liked the 'cop to cop' part.

They turned and resumed walking. "We both have trouble believing that Padruig Nessmith is the killer," he started.

"What about the traffic cam footage?" she asked.

"At best, it's circumstantial, and he has an excuse for driving to Asheville. That's why the judge let him out on bail."

She nodded her agreement. "Pretty thin stuff when you think about it.

"Yes, but it was enough to wind Curry up, and then the Feds insisted he stick to Nessmith as the prime suspect and make it public. They think it will give them cover to catch a Russkiy hit team they believe was after Davis." He snorted in derision. "Russkiy hit team. Craziest thing I ever heard. Damn Feds are nuts!"

She couldn't help but agree, given her experience and her general attitude toward the Federal Government and its minions. Nevertheless, she had to admit that the "Feds" had pulled her bacon out of the fire a few times. And this made her think of Strachey. *How would Bob handle this situation?*

"And?" she asked. "Where does that leave you?"

"That's what I'm asking you." Those sharp eyes raked across her face again, caught her eyes and held them. "I have a feeling you guys have made more progress. Anything the police might do is stymied by those gummint boys' orders to stand pat on Nessmith."

"You're confirming that the Feds are willing to sacrifice Padruig while they run around in circles?"

Wolf grimaced and nodded. "And while we're stuck in a holding pattern the case gets colder by the minute."

"Why doesn't Curry tell the Feds to piss off?"

He grimaced. "In many ways Curry is a good guy. Normally, he'd be full steam ahead. But he tends to defer to the kind of authority the CIA and FBI wield. And there's local political pressure, as well. Nobody seems to like Padruig Nessmith. The mayor is a member of Jaidon Nessmith's country club."

Despite his words, Krystal wondered if Curry, frustrated by the hold the Feds had put on his investigation, had sent Wolf to see her. There was no way she could be sure, but she could guess what was coming next.

"So," said Wolf, "is there anything you can tell me about what you've found out? Is there something we're missing that would break the logjam?"

She wasn't about to tell him anything about Yang and the bank documents. In any event, she needed to consult with Strachey and the team on this development. "We're still pursuing our own line of inquiry," she said carefully.

Wolf interrupted her. "So, you've identified a third suspect besides Nessmith and the Russkies?"

Wolf was quick. He was a good cop, and this made her want to trust him, but she couldn't, not yet.

"I didn't say that," she said. "There's really nothing more I can say right now."

Disappointment flooded his face. "I understand," he said. "I probably wouldn't trust me either if I were in your shoes. Still, I want to stay in touch. I might be able to help you, or *vice versa*. Talk it over with your boss, er 'partner,' and let's meet again. I contacted you because you used to be a cop. I want to solve this case, and I hope I didn't make a mistake coming to you. Here." He held out a business card. "I wrote my cell number on the back. Call me any time of night or day."

They walked back to the parking lot where Wolf paused before getting into his car. "One thing," he said, "Not even the Feds believe it was Nessmith. If the killer was really after Davis, Russian or not, then Nessmith's alleged motive doesn't work. And if the killer wasn't Russian, then we and the feds are looking in the wrong place. But maybe you've already come to that conclusion."

Krystal watched him drive away in his muddy Jeep. *He must do some off-roading in that thing.* It said something about Wolf being a risk taker, and she liked that. And he was smart.

CHAPTER 26

Krystal drove straight to Strachey's house. She arrived just as they were sitting down to dinner, and Amy insisted she join them in a true Southern meal of fried chicken, mashed potatoes and gravy, and corn on the cob. Thomas Jefferson Dawson watched pridefully as his grandson worked diligently on a corn cob. Robert Thomas had adopted the "typewriter" technique.

"That's my boy," beamed Thomas Jefferson, "just look at him go after that corn."

"Daddy," said Amy with a smile that belied the admonition, "it's not polite to comment on the eating habits of others at the table."

Her father pretended to be offended. "I'm just admiring my grandson's skill," he said. "Ain't he efficient, though? There won't be a kernel left on that cob when he's done with it."

Robert Thomas paused in his demolition of the corn to look at his grandfather. "Papaw, you said 'ain't' again."

"Oh," said Thomas Jefferson, "I'm sorry. I just keep forgettin' my grammar."

Robert Thomas nodded sagely, apparently satisfied with his grandfather's response, and resumed attacking the corn.

The meal was completed with apple pie, and Krystal, Amy, and Strachey retired to the living room while Thomas Jefferson took his grandson upstairs to prepare for bed.

Strachey was anxious to hear about the meeting with Wolf and leaned forward, hands on knees to listen to Krystal's account. When she had finished, he stood and walked to a side table where he opened a large, burled walnut humidor and withdrew a postprandial cigar. He clipped the cap and held a match to the foot before taking a draw of fragrant smoke. Krystal and Amy waited for him to speak, both aware that it would be a *faux pas* to interrupt the ritual.

"This is downright interesting," he said after resuming his seat. "Do you think Curry sent him, or was he telling you the truth?"

Krystal frowned. "I can't be sure. He seemed sincere, but he's a cop, which means he follows orders."

"That wasn't always the case with you," smiled Strachey.

"I always had a good reason."

"Maybe Wolf has a good reason, too."

"So, you think we should trust him ... tell him about Wang and the bank thing?"

He shook his head. "Not yet, but we might need an ally in the police before this is over. There has to be somebody to make an arrest."

"An arrest seems like wishful thinking at this point. So far, we've got nothing that would pin the murder on Yang."

Amy had said nothing until now. "But according to the bank documents Wang is breaking the law, isn't he?"

"He's breaking some kind of law, for sure," said Strachey, "and he's stealing from the bank. But some of it is quite abstruse. Double bookkeeping is certainly against the rules of any honest business. I'm sure there is a list of federal banking regulations he's broken, apart from the theft. In and of itself, what we've discovered could hurt the bank big time and probably cause a terrific scandal if it becomes public. There is plenty of motive for murder there, but so far, we've found nothing provable apart from the financial crimes."

"You still don't think Pushkin was attempting to blackmail Yang?" asked Krystal, recalling Amy's earlier speculation. "He brought the evidence home and apparently hid what he'd discovered from his boss, Kim Stevens. That's a little strange, isn't it, if Pushkin didn't have blackmail in mind?"

"Yeah. Why would he hide something like this from his boss? It's something to keep in mind," agreed Strachey. "Maybe ..." He paused in mid-sentence as if a thought had struck him.

Amy could read him like a book. "OK, out with it. What are you thinking?"

"Well," he started, "maybe we should shake the tree, see what falls out. The longer this drags on, the worst it is for Padruig."

Krystal gave him a wary look. "OK," she said, "what do you have in mind?"

"Look, nothing's happening, right? We could watch Yang for a year and not find anything. He has no reason to deviate from the norm now that Pushkin is out of the way. Padruig is the very public prime suspect, and behind the scenes, the feebies and spooks have put everything else on hold. Wolf confirmed it."

"Right," she nodded. *He's about to propose another spook idea,* she thought.

"I can guess what you're thinking, but just hear me out. So, even if Pushkin wasn't trying on some blackmail, he was in a position to do so. Given Yang's phone call to him before the murder, Yang knew he had something, and he was none too pleased about it."

Amy and Krystal nodded their agreement.

"So," he continued while trying to gauge their reaction, "even if Pushkin wasn't blackmailing Yang, maybe we could."

Krystal and Amy stared at him for a few beats, their expressions unreadable. Strachey's cigar had gone out, and he fussed with it, knocking the ash off into a large crystal ashtray and re-lighting it with another wooden match. He shook the match out and asked, "What do you think?"

Amy asked, "And how do you propose we go about this exactly?"

"We could call him and make some threats," he said through a cloud of blue smoke

"Who could call him?" asked Amy.

Krystal still wasn't sold on the idea. "But I thought you agreed we shouldn't step over the line."

"Well," said Strachey defensively, "I can't think of anything better. Can you? We're running out of time to figure this thing out. Our client might actually be arraigned and put on trial. There's no telling how deep the feds can reach into Charlotte's justice system."

Strachey was now puffing furiously on his cigar making the tip burn bright orange. "What if," he continued, "Natasha Pushkin called him and threatened to expose his scam?"

"He must know Pushkin had the incriminating documents," said Amy. "Otherwise he wouldn't have called Pushkin."

Strachey nodded. "Like we said, Yang has a lot to lose – a hundred million."

"We can't get close to Natasha," said Krystal.

"The Feds are all over her, probably have her house surrounded now with instructions to shoot Robert Strachey on sight. And Yang knows the incriminating files are encrypted. He probably feels safe."

"Right you are," he said. "But he would still want to get his hands on them. And it doesn't necessarily have to be Natasha herself who calls. Amy can fake a pretty good Russian accent. And if Yang gets any murderous ideas about Natasha, he'd have to fight his way through a security cordon. Natasha's safety is not a concern."

Amy had been thinking about her husband's idea. "You think 'Natasha' should demand a blackmail payment. If he pays without trying to kill her, it would mean he's not our murderer."

"Not necessarily, but something like that," he said.

Krystal still was not satisfied. "Even if he pays up or shows up with gun, what are we supposed to do? We can't arrest him."

"There may be a way around that," said Strachey.

CHAPTER 27

On weekends Raymond Yang liked to spend time with his kids, twins - a boy and a girl - 10 years old. Soon, he knew, they would enter that stage of life when children become rebellious and begin to think their parents are ogres. Raymond intended to enjoy their childhood before they grew out of it. This Saturday morning, they had planned a full day at his country club, Quail Hollow. He'd play a round of golf while his wife and the twins enjoyed the pool, followed by the Saturday buffet.

Life was good except for THE THING, which hovered ever in the back of his mind, a dark backdrop that often could be glimpsed through the scenery as though everything else was an artificial construct. At times he felt like a high wire walker on a rubber band, and it had become worse over the past month.

The family returned home, exhausted at 4:00 PM. The twins were squirmy and quarrelsome with fatigue. Yang's wife, Susan, led them to the entertainment room and put some cartoons on the 100-inch flat screen, then returned to the living room where Yang had flopped into an overstuffed chair. "Raymond," she said, "you're still in your sweaty golf clothes. Why don't you go up and take a nice shower? I'll have a pitcher of martinis waiting when you come back down."

He didn't feel like going upstairs. He knew his wife meant well, but it still felt like nagging. He didn't feel like moving, at all. His golf had been atrocious, ending with a score in the nineties, way above his average. It had put him in a bad mood which had persisted throughout the day.

"You've hardly spoken since lunch," said Susan. "Is something the matter?"

"Lousy golf today," he mumbled.

"Well, next time will be better. Now go take a shower and put on some fresh things. It might help. Golf is not that important, you know."

"The hell it isn't," he growled. But he stood and made for the stairs.

The hot water coursing over his body did make him feel better. He closed his eyes and let it pour over him for a full five minutes, twisting the temperature knob to its highest setting. *There have been no repercussions yet, and weeks have passed. Everyone is convinced the old tightwad took out his brother and sister-in-law over some ancient feud that hardly anyone even remembers. Regrettable in many ways, but still a stroke of luck that they were there. The diversion of attention away from Davis was an unexpected benefit.*

He stepped out of the shower and dried himself with a soft, Egyptian cotton towel, wrapped it around his waist and wiped the fog from the mirror over the sink. The face he saw was emotionless. A*s cold as my mother-in-law's heart,* he thought as his lips twisted into a nasty sneer. For once he felt fortunate to have an inscrutable Oriental face. He looked at his hands. They weren't shaking. *Good.*

He pulled on a loose-fitting jogging outfit and went downstairs where Susan, true to her word, had an ice-cold pitcher of martinis waiting. She poured him one, and he downed it in one swallow.

"Take it easy," exclaimed Susan.

"Thirsty," he said, and held out the martini glass for more as he chewed on the olives.

"You should have a glass of water, then," she said, nevertheless obediently filling his glass. "At this rate you won't be in any condition to have dinner with the kids."

He glared at her over the rim of his glass and defiantly swallowed half of the ice-cold gin.

Susan gave up. Her husband was in one of his moods, which had become more frequent and darker. Something was bothering him, but no matter how hard she tried, he would tell her nothing. Now he was turning to drink to calm whatever demons were eating at him. Maybe there was trouble at the office. She'd hoped that a day at the club with the twins would mellow him out, but he was sinking into another depression, and she decided her best course of action right now was to leave him alone. She carried her untouched martini into the kitchen and poured it down the drain.

At 6:00 PM Raymond Yang had not moved from his chair. The martini pitcher on the table beside him was empty, and the water which had condensed on its outer surface had long since slid down to make a puddle on the tabletop. His mind, at last, was a fuzzy blank.

This hard-won tranquility was broken by the jangle of the phone which jolted him out of his fugue. He stared blearily at the source of the disturbance, which sat on an occasional table on the other side of the room. Given the rate at which the room was now spinning there was no possibility that he could traverse the space to the phone without risking a fall, so he could only sit there as the noise drove nails through brain.

At last, the ringing stopped, and he closed his eyes trying to withdraw back into the shelter of the fog. But Susan came down the stairs. "Raymond, it's for you. Some woman with an accent."

She had answered the phone upstairs.

He managed to say, "I don't want to speak to anyone right now. Tell them to call back."

Susan gave him an intent look that quickly turned to disgust. She recognized the symptoms. She'd placed the call on hold on the upstairs phone. "You'll have to tell them yourself," she said in a sudden burst of anger. "I won't make excuses for you." She lifted the cordless receiver and spoke into it. "Just a moment, please. I'll put him right on."

Yang glared at his wife. "At least ask who it is," he mumbled.

Susan did so. Putting her hand over the microphone she said, "She says her name is Natalie Davis."

An electric shock passed through Yang's body, and he thought for a moment that he might vomit. Instead, he passed out.

Susan glared at him as she raised the phone to her ear. Making her voice normal with an effort, she said, "I'm sorry, but he simply can't speak with anyone right now. May I take a message?" She listened to the response and said, "Very well. You should call back, then."

She replaced the phone in its cradle with a final angry glance at her husband turned and stalked back up the stairs. She had made sandwiches for the kids to eat in front of the TV, and soon it would be time to tuck them into bed. Raymond, as far as she was concerned, could lay in his chair the rest of the evening and all night. *Maybe my mother is right about him.* Her mother had always thought there was something off about Yang, which Susan had put to racial prejudice until now.

*****

Amy would use a burner phone, and except for Krystal, they were all gathered around Strachey's desk at PSI. There was general disappointment when Amy ended the call without speaking to Yang. Krystal was posted down the street from the Yang house in case the call prompted him to make some sort of move. A non-response was the last thing they had expected.

"So, what the hell do we do when he just refuses to take the call?" asked Amy.

Despite the initial failure Strachey could not repress a chuckle. "Yeah, what happens when the mark just refuses to talk to us? We'll try again tomorrow morning when he's most likely to be available. I'll call Krystal and tell her go home and get some rest."

Krystal was disappointed. She'd looked forward to watching a panicked Yang run out of his house and maybe contact a partner in crime or make a run for the airport. The evening, having lost its purpose now faded to black and stretched ahead like a road through a featureless landscape. She could go home and park in front of the TV, but she did not want to be alone.

Being alone risked drowning in her own thoughts. She'd never confronted this difficulty before because she had been too busy pursuing a career in police work, and then Ray had come along and given her more.

Michael R. Davidson

She sat there, gripped by indecision as her earlier enthusiasm evaporated leaving her feeling like a stale Coke left out overnight. She had a wild thought of going to a bar and picking up a man but discarded it as another manifestation of self-loathing. *Should I buy a plane ticket and fly to Miami. Beg forgiveness of Ray?* Her pride instantly overrode the thought. *Pull yourself together! It's not the end of the world.*

In the end, she drove home and dug an unopened bottle of scotch out of the kitchen cabinet.

CHAPTER 28

Strachey called Krystal early Sunday morning and was surprised when she didn't answer. He tried several more times, becoming increasingly frustrated. "Where the hell could she be?" he asked Amy. "There's work to do."

"Maybe she went out for groceries or something."

"She knew we were set to call Yang again this morning, and we need her in place for surveillance. It's not like her to crap out on a job."

"Do you think something's wrong?"

"I don't know." He shook his head, worried. "But I don't want to wait any longer. I'll drive over to Yang's house myself. I'll phone as soon as I get there, and you can make the call."

They had worked out a script for Amy to use, something they hoped would flush Yang into the open if he were the killer. It was after 10:30 AM when she finally dialed the number. Once again, Mrs. Yang answered the phone. And this time, after a short delay, Raymond Yang himself was on the line. "Who's calling?" he asked.

Such calls as Amy made to Yang have a common form and hew to certain rules. *I know what you did, and it was wrong and illegal. I'll tell the police unless you pay me X amount of money. Here is how I want to receive the payment.* In this instance, Amy, impersonating Natasha Pushkin, said she had the files her husband had brought home and knew what they contained. She also said she was certain Yang had murdered her husband. She demanded one million dollars in cash to remain silent.

Yang's response was at first to deny that he had done anything wrong, but he seemed out of breath, as though someone had punched him in the stomach. "No matter what you think," he said, "I didn't murder anybody."

"I will give you a little time to think about it, Mr. Yang," concluded Amy. "But just a little time. I will call you back this evening." She pressed the end call button on the burner phone before he could answer.

*****

Yang did feel like he'd been punched in the stomach. He stood there in his living room staring at the dead phone in his hand, still in the track suit he'd donned the evening before, frozen in place. Stricken by *l'esprit de l'escalier*, he wished in retrospect that he had had the wit to demand proof of what the woman said. The troublesome files were encrypted, and it was entirely possible all she had was a bunch of data she could not decipher. In fact, the Davis woman had offered no proof that she had an inkling of what was in the files. The worst thing had been the accusation of murder. He cursed himself. When she called again, he would have some questions for her. She would not control the conversation or him. It was comforting to think he might be able to handle the situation. If not, he had options.

He changed into street clothes and left the house before his wife had a chance to ask where he was going.

*****

Strachey missed Yang's departure. He returned home at Amy's request because she was worried about their friend. "Bob, I'm worried about Krystal. I've tried calling several times, both to her apartment and to her cell, but there's no answer. Do you think something could have happened to her?"

"Do you think we should drive over there?"

"I just feel that something's wrong," she said. "Yes, let's go over."

Krystal's car was in the parking lot of her apartment building in Southpark. They looked at one another, concern reflected in their faces. When they got no response from knocking on her door, Amy used the spare key Krystal had given her.

The sun shot horizontal rays across the living room and over the supine body of Krystal Murphy, sprawled face-up on the sofa, her mouth gaping open, and an empty scotch bottle and glass lying on the floor beside her dangling arm.

Strachey and Amy looked at one another in alarm. "Christ," whispered Strachey into his wife's ear, "she's had a relapse." A little over a year ago Krystal's flirtation with alcoholism had brought her very near disaster. She had said nothing to Strachey and Amy, but they had read the signs. To their gratification, she had pulled herself out of it and had seemed perfectly normal. She still drank, but only socially and never over the limit. *Until I opened that bottle of Lagavulin in the office,* he thought and mentally kicked himself for enticing her into overindulgence. Guilt rose in him like bitter bile.

"She's been very unhappy, Bob," said Amy. "I

think it's more than the break-up with her boyfriend. I'm afraid she has some real issues, the kind of issues that require professional help."

Strachey was shocked. He had thought Krystal's dark moods were a temporary phenomenon, a reaction to the break-up. Normal people got over such things. They moved on with their lives. But Krystal was not getting better, and the thought occurred that perhaps the break-up was a manifestation of her problem rather than the cause.

Amy knelt beside the sofa and gently shook Krystal by the shoulder while speaking in a soft voice. "Krystal, wake up, honey. It's Bob and Amy."

With a groan Krystal's eyes opened a slit but remained unfocused. She tried to raise her head, but only groaned again, this time more loudly, as she fell back. Amy turned to Strachey. "Help me get her into the bedroom, then go to the kitchen and brew a pot of coffee."

They hoisted a semi-conscious Krystal to her feet and managed to get her into the bedroom where they laid her on the bed, which had not been slept in. "She must have come home yesterday and immediately started drinking," said Amy. "Go away. I'm going to undress her and try to get her into the shower. I'll call if I need help."

Strachey was not anxious to participate in getting a naked Krystal into the shower, thinking of the embarrassment it would cause her later, if she remembered. "Please, don't call me unless it's absolutely necessary," he said and headed for the kitchen.

A half-hour later Amy led Krystal into the kitchen

to a chair. She was fully awake now, but her eyes were bloodshot and her face pale with a tinge of green. Her auburn hair was wet, and she was wrapped in a thick terrycloth robe. She avoided looking at Strachey when he placed a cup of black coffee in front of her.

"She needs something solid in her stomach," said Amy.

"I'll make some buttered toast." Strachey found the bread and the toaster and a few minutes later set a plate in front of Krystal who just stared at it for a beat before sighing deeply and taking a small bite. Even in this condition, thought Strachey, she's an incredibly beautiful young woman. It was hard for him to understand what demons might have driven her to such self-destructive behavior.

Krystal took another half-hearted bite of toast, still refusing to look at Strachey. Without warning, her face collapsed, and her shoulders heaved with wracking sobs as tears poured down her face. "I'm sorry," she breathed, "I'm sorry and so ashamed."

Strachey and Amy both knelt beside her and wrapped their arms around her shoulders. Strachey was profoundly touched, and his voice caught in his throat. "It's all right, Krystal," he said. "We're here for you."

"There must be something wrong with me," gasped Krystal between sobs. "This isn't right."

"We'll see you through this," said Amy, more in control of her emotions than her husband. "We're not going to leave you alone."

When Krystal had regained her composure, Amy called home and told her father that Strachey would stop by for a moment to gather some things, but they would not return home that night. Not for the first time, she was grateful her father was living with them.

Krystal managed to get the rest of the toast down but could not face the coffee. Amy found some tomato juice in the refrigerator. "You need to rehydrate," she said. "Drink all of this you can and maybe some water. I'll see if you have any aspirin. Then, I want you to lie down in your bed until you feel better."

CHAPTER 29

Raymond Yang had had time to gather his thoughts in the wake of the Sunday morning phone call. It had set him on his heels, and he had stammered like a schoolboy when the threats and demands were made. Now, after cool reflection, he thought he knew how to handle the situation. Natalie Davis was probably bluffing. She had to be bluffing. There was no way she had decrypted those files.

He was nervous when Sunday evening finally came, and it must have showed because his wife was concerned. "Is everything all right?" she asked. She'd made a family favorite, roast beef and mashed potatoes for dinner. The twins were enthusiastically stuffing their mouths while Yang shoved the food around his plate untouched.

"Of course," he replied, eyes fixed on his plate. "Just some stuff at work."

"You should leave work at the office," said Susan. "You need to relax weekends. Why don't you take tomorrow off, and we could take a drive in the country?"

He barely heard her and grunted noncommittally. She stood with hands on hips for a few moments before busying herself clearing the plates. She thought she might take the twins to visit her mother. Her husband had been uncommunicative and grumpy since Friday evening, and she had had enough. *Let him sit and stew in his own juices,* she thought. Yang didn't even notice when she and the children left him alone at the table.

He waited. It was 9:00 PM before the phone rang.

Michael R. Davidson

He let it ring a few times before picking up the receiver.

*****

Amy finished the call with a feeling of satisfaction. Yang had tried to stymie her by saying he knew the files were encrypted. "If they actually contain anything incriminating," he said, "you could never break the code."

Her response had been immediate and devastating for Yang. "Well, then, do you suppose the authorities won't be interested in Emerald Trading and the hundred million dollars you've siphoned into that account in the Cayman Islands? All of that double bookkeeping must have been exhausting for you."

After a stunned silence, he'd asked, "What do you want?"

She repeated the demand for one million dollars. "And I want it in cash," she'd added.

He said it would take some time to gather such a sum, and she gave him two days, saying she would call again Tuesday evening to tell him how to deliver the money.

"We need to find a place for the exchange," said Strachey. Amy had filled him in on the conversation with Yang.

"I agree," she replied, "but there are other things to think about. We've kind of rushed into this thing, and I don't know what you're thinking."

"I think that if Yang is the killer, he may try to repeat his performance. That's why we're going to need Krystal." He had no intention of putting his wife in the line of fire. Krystal was experienced and knew how to handle herself despite her problems.

That their efforts could end in violence had been obvious to Amy, and she was frightened, but there was another possibility. "What if Yang isn't the killer and he just shows up with a bag of money expecting to get his files back? You're betting a lot that he was responsible for the murders."

"You're right. There are two possible outcomes: he's a killer, and he'll try it again, or he's just a crook. If he's just a crook, we'll have to turn the evidence over to the police."

"You want Krystal to play the part of Natasha at the meeting." The idea worried her.

"Yes. She'll be armed, and she's experienced. And she won't be alone. I'll be there with my gun drawn and trained on Yang in case he gets the drop on her."

"There will be a lot of explaining to do," she said, now more concerned than ever, "no matter how it turns out. I don't like any of it. Maybe we should go to the police now and let them handle it."

He shook his head. "We can't count on Curry's cooperation. And he's been warned off by our Federal friends."

"They can't ignore the evidence."

"Of course, they can. They're feds. Curry might bring him in for questioning, but the murders won't be resolved that way. He might willingly serve a jail term for financial fraud, but he'll never volunteer that he is a murderer."

She could not disagree with his logic. "So, we're stuck with this wild hare plan, and you're determined to put Krystal in harm's way."

CHAPTER 30

It was dark. She lay there squeezing her eyes closed in the soft comfort and safety of the bed and the warmth of the blankets. At first, she was confused, remembering sitting in her car outside Yang's house. What happened next was like something concealed behind a semi-transparent veil that she could pierce only if she concentrated. She remembered coming home and pulling the bottle from its hiding place in the cabinet, then the first drink and another and another until there was no memory. Then more confusion until the cold water of the shower hit her and the pain and nausea began. She remembered embarrassment and crying like she had not cried since she was a child, and tears started from her eyes again and rolled down the sides of her face onto the pillow. Desperation to regain control seized her, and she shut her eyes tight, concentrating on restoring order to her thoughts.

She didn't know how long she lay there unmoving until she shoved the covers aside and sat up on the edge of the bed. She was still wearing the terrycloth robe and discovered she was naked beneath it, as naked as she felt before the forces that buffeted her like a strong wind in a storm against which she had to struggle to move forward. She went into the bathroom, switched on the light and looked at herself in the mirror. Staring back at her was a pale face surrounded by a tangle of still damp auburn hair, but worst of all was the frightened expression, and fright was an emotion she had adamantly exiled.

She could hear the television from the living

room and realized someone was out there. It must be Strachey and Amy. She had no idea what time it was, and her watch was missing from her wrist. She found it lying on a night table and saw that it was nearing midnight.

She didn't want to face her friends, but she couldn't hide in the bedroom forever. Screwing up her courage, she dressed quickly in jeans and a t-shirt and walked out to the living room.

Amy turned at her entrance. Strachey's head rested against the back of his chair, and she could see he was asleep. Amy had been watching an episode of a British mystery series, and she switched the television off when Krystal entered. She stood and smiled. "Feeling better?" she asked.

"Nearly human," said Krystal and suddenly realized she was hungry. "I'm going to make a sandwich," she said, and turned toward the kitchen.

Amy followed. "Let's let Bob sleep. "He's had a long day, and he's terribly worried about you. Do you feel like talking?"

Krystal found a package of baloney and some cheese in the refrigerator and set about constructing a sandwich. *Do I feel like talking?* What did she have to say, really? That her life was a mess, and she didn't know why? How could she express how she felt? She had spent most of her adult life suppressing her emotions, fearful that in her male-dominated profession emotions would make her weak, vulnerable to misogynistic criticism of being "soft." So, she had locked her emotions away to be brought out occasionally in private moments and viewed like family jewels in a lockbox. In a flash of revelation, she again recognized a kinship between herself and Padruig Nessmith.

She stopped working on the sandwich and turned to face Amy. "I think I do need to talk to someone," she said. "I guess you're elected."

"Make a sandwich for me, too," said Amy, "then sit down here at the table with me."

Sitting across the table from Amy, she felt that if she did not lower her defenses now, she would burst. "I'm not very good with emotions," she began.

*****

"We should leave her alone today," said Amy. She and Strachey were driving home. It was 4:00 AM. "She has a lot to think about, maybe some personal reassessment to do."

"Tell me all about it tomorrow, er, today or whenever," yawned Strachey. "Let's catch a little shut-eye. I'm exhausted."

"Bob, you slept most of the night. You were sawing logs."

"I'm emotionally distressed."

She smacked him on the shoulder. "That's not funny."

"Guess not," he said. "You think she'll be OK?"

"Well, I'm no expert, but last night was cathartic for her. It's something that's been building for a long time. But your plan to use her to entrap Yang worries me."

"What about the booze?" he asked. Another bout with a bottle and his plan would go up in smoke.

She looked out the window. There had been a

light rain in the night, and the streets were wet. "I don't know," she said. "Alcohol is an escape for her, but I suppose that can be said of almost any alcoholic."

"So, you think she's an alcoholic?" He was feeling guilty again for drinking with her in the office, especially the episode with the expensive scotch.

She shook her head. "Like I said, I'm no expert. That's something for a specialist to decide. I think she needs psychotherapy to work everything out. She has real issues, and they're snapping at her heels like a pack of wolves right now."

Strachey said, "It must have been the break-up with her boyfriend that triggered it."

"Whatever it was, it burst the dam. She's going to need us."

"That goes without saying."

He drove on for a while, the tires making hissing sounds against the wet pavement. "Do you think she's still able to work?" he asked.

"We'll see. She seemed OK when we left. I think our talk did some good. But we shouldn't push her."

"You're right, of course, but a lot depends on her right now."

Could he in all good conscience ask her to do this? Krystal would risk injury or worse if things went bad. He knew she would accept the risk without question, perhaps even welcome it. But, still her safety might in the end depend entirely on Strachey's own skills.

There was a contingency he had been holding in reserve, and as he lay awake next to his wife, he turned it over in his mind again and again.

CHAPTER 31

Krystal had shown Amy the two remaining bottles of scotch in the kitchen cabinet and asked her to take them away. It was a first step. The rest of Monday she would take off, find something mindless to watch on TV, and prepare herself for the rendezvous with Yang the following night. Strangely, though she was alone again with her thoughts, escape into a bottle held no charm. She had succumbed three times over the past week, and it could not continue.

The plan for Tuesday night kept her mind occupied. Action, she thought, was the antidote to what ailed her. She half hoped Yang would charge her with gun blazing.

It was nearing noon when her cell phone rang. It was Wolf. "Can you meet me right away? I can't get away from the office for long, and I'm on my lunch break."

Wolf's voice was pregnant with suppressed excitement.

"OK, she said," suddenly pleased to have an excuse to get out of the apartment. "Where are you?"

"You live near Southpark Mall, don't you?"

"Yes." It was interesting that he knew where she lived.

"Meet me at Paco's Tacos in ten minutes."

"Um, OK." She exchanged her T-shirt for a bra and cotton blouse, combed out her hair, and headed for her car.

Wolf was already at a table in the restaurant when she arrived. He waved her to join him. "I ordered some cokes and tacos," he said, "to save time. I have to get back to the office before Curry gets curious."

"What's up?"

"It seems the shit has hit the fan with Natalie Davis."

Krystal thought immediately that somehow the cops had learned of Amy Strachey's impersonation of Natasha.

"How so?" she asked cautiously.

Wolf gave her a long look, which worried her even more.

"Someone took a shot at her last night," he said.

She sat in stunned silence for a few beats before she realized that her jaw was hanging open.

Wolf continued, "I thought you should know. The Feds are all over themselves, more certain than ever that the Russians are behind it."

"Tell me what happened. When did it happen? Was anyone hurt?" The questions tumbled out of her.

"It was around nine PM last night. Mrs. Davis and a CIA security guy – they replaced that girl – were in the kitchen, and a shot came through the window narrowly missing Mrs. Davis. The bullet came from a high-powered rifle. The security guy stayed on top of Mrs. Davis in case a hit team charged in and called for back-up. The entire neighborhood was locked down within ten minutes, but whoever fired the shot got away clean. They're tamping down news of the incident and the Feds have taken Mrs. Davis to a safe site."

She tried to come up with an appropriate response, but all she could say was, "Holy shit!"

"Yeah," he said, "Looks like we were wrong to ignore the Russian angle."

She was thinking fast. What did this mean for their plans to entrap Yang? She was on the verge of telling everything to Wolf but bit her tongue.

"I've got to let Strachey know about this. I'm still not sure I can believe it. The idea of a Russian assassin is just too damned far-fetched. You're sure it was nine PM?" she asked.

"Absolutely. Why do you ask?" His eyes turned a darker shade of blue when his curiosity was piqued.

"Nothing," she said hastily. "I just want to be sure I had the facts straight. I really appreciate your telling me about this," she said. "Frankly, I don't know where we go from here. What about Padruig?"

He shook his head. "The Feds don't want Curry to cut him loose until they can sort things out. I'm sorry."

"I know," she said. "Thanks again, Wolf, but I have to let Strachey know what happened." She was already getting to her feet.

Call me Archie," he said.

She shot him a nervous smile over her shoulder and left just as the tacos arrived at the table.

She drove as fast as she could to PSI and burst into Strachey's office out of breath. "You're not gonna believe this," she panted.

When she was finished, he called Amy into the office and had her repeat the story.

Strachey was non-plussed. "I can't believe the Russians would pull a stunt like that on American soil."

"Tell that to the Brits," said Amy.

"The Russians don't usually take potshots with rifles in these situations," said Strachey. "Poison is their preferred method."

"Maybe," replied Amy, "but they knew Natasha was being protected. Maybe they got desperate. Maybe it was success or Lefortovo. You know how they are."

Strachey scratched his chin. "My first thought was that Yang tried to take her out after those first phone calls, but the attack was at nine o'clock, the same time you had him on the phone."

"That kind of narrows down the possibilities, doesn't it?" asked Krystal.

Strachey's expression was sour. "Yeah, I guess it does."

"So," asked Amy, "what are we going to do now about Yang?"

"We can't let him get away with what he's done," said Krystal. Her cop instincts were kicking in.

"We have gone to all this trouble," said Amy.

"So," asked Strachey, all his enthusiasm gone, "what do you want to do."

"I have an idea," said Krystal.

CHAPTER 32

Krystal wore jeans, a polo shirt, and sneakers and a black wig that tickled her scalp. Freedom Park is large with a lot of trees that offere good cover. There is a pond at the south end with a cement walk around its border. It's a large pond, about three and a half football fields long and over 300 feet wide. She was at the north end on an arched stone bridge that led from the shore to a small island. She stood at the eastern end of the bridge where it joined the bank.

There was no lighting in this area, and a waxing moon which shone through a skein of feathery clouds provided the only illumination, leaving deep shadows under the trees. A brook known as Sugar Creek ran parallel to the eastern bank of the pond, set back about thirty feet through a screen of trees. Strachey was out there somewhere providing overwatch.

If Yang was desperate enough to try something violent, Krystal was not particularly concerned. She was packing her faithful Beretta Px4Storm, a formidable .45 caliber weapon, in a holster at the small of her back concealed by the loose tail of her shirt.

Yang had been given precise instructions to park along Princeton Avenue at the south end of the pond and walk north around the pond to the bridge where "Natalie" would be waiting. This would bring him into the open some distance from Krystal so he could be observed as he approached along the cement walk. The rendezvous was set for eleven P.M. when the park should be empty. It was a deliberately provocative scenario which gave Yang ample opportunity to try a hostile move.

She almost hoped he would try something. The adrenalin and other forces that had been building inside left her feeling like a balloon inflated beyond capacity. The cool night air felt good against her skin, and she was thankful for it, but action would provide a better release. She was glad to be here, oh so grateful, that Strachey still trusted her. He and Amy had seen the worst, vulnerabilities she'd hoped no one would ever see. But the experience had not driven them away.

In the distance occasional cars passed along Princeton Avenue. She'd cased the area earlier in the day and knew there was space to park along the shoulder where Yang was to arrive. It was hard to see that far through the gloom, but she knew Strachey would be positioned to see his arrival.

She saw movement, and there was just enough moonlight for her to make out a figure emerging onto the walk from the direction of the road. Her watch told her it was precisely eleven P.M. Yang was right on time like a good accountant. The figure moved to its right to follow the walkway along the eastern bank of the pond. She could not make out if he was carrying anything. A million dollars in cash made quite a bundle. She waited, her muscles tensing for action. She wondered if he had ever met Natasha Pushkin.

She followed Yang's progress as he moved from dim, silvery light to shadow. At this distance and in this light, she could not even be sure it was Yang. It took longer than she expected for him to traverse the distance to the path leading onto the bridge, suggesting he was in no hurry to consummate the meeting. He carried a paper shopping bag in his left hand.

When he was within five feet of her, he raised his right hand, and something metallic glinted in the moonlight. She snaked her arm behind her back to draw the Beretta, but he was too fast. She was dazzled by an excruciatingly bright light. Yang was using a flashlight with a high lumen count to blind her.

She took a quick step back, trying to shield her eyes, expecting him to attack, but instead he backed away, keeping the light trained on her. A second later she heard a sharp report from her left, and a piece of stone from the bridge chipped with a high-pitched twang as a bullet ricocheted off it. She dove for cover behind the waist-level parapet shaking her head to ward off the temporary blindness while she drew her Beretta. She rolled against the parapet struggling to see Yang through the shimmering white haze in front of her eyes. She knew she was helpless, a perfect target.

He was still shining the light on her, but when she drew the pistol, he turned and ran full tilt back the way he'd come. She shook her head as sight returned, leaving bright spots dancing before her eyes.

There was still a shooter somewhere north of the bridge with a high-powered rifle. What had happened was clear in an instant. Yang had a confederate waiting for him to light her up so he could get a clear shot. The question now was whether the shooter was still out there somewhere in the dark waiting for another opportunity. She didn't dare expose herself to chase Yang who was running like a scalded dog.

CHAPTER 33

Robert Strachey kept to the trees beside the walkway and was close enough to recognize Raymond Yang as he walked slowly toward Krystal. He silently paralleled the banker as he approached the bridge. It was too dark to see much more than that the man was carrying a paper shopping bag presumably filled with money. He had a sinking feeling that he was going to pay the blackmail and walk away, leaving them no closer to identifying the real killer.

As Yang approached the bridge Strachey was some twenty feet away, concealed in the trees. This was the moment Yang would either reveal himself as a murderer or walk away having convicted himself of bank fraud. When Yang was a few feet from Krystal he made a quick movement with something in his hand. There was a bright light, and simultaneously he recognized the report of a high-powered rifle and saw Krystal fall to the ground. *Shit! She's been hit.* And every doubt he had had about placing her in such a position flooded his brain.

Yang began to run back the way he had come. Strachey was torn between going after Yang and checking on Krystal, but she yelled, "Get him. I'm OK."

Yang had gained a lead on him, but Strachey's old talents on the football field came into play, and by the time they had covered about half the distance along the walkway, he tackled the fleeing banker to the ground and pinned his arms behind him. Strachey was breathing heavily, and Yang gasped for breath.

In the distance there was another report from the

rifle answered by several more shots.

Still concerned for Krystal, Strachey hauled Yang to his feet and shoved him back toward the bridge. Krystal was still hunkered down next to the parapet and brought her pistol quickly to bear on them. "Whoa, Krystal, it's me," he said. "Are you OK?"

"Yeah, they missed me. You better get down here." With a glare at the exhausted Yang, she said, "You can leave him standing up." She jerked her head in the direction of the gunshots. "What the hell's going on out there? Sounds like a shooting gallery."

Strachey's teeth flashed in the moonlight. "That must be our insurance policy."

They listened, but there was no more gunfire. "We'd better get up there," said Strachey. "Do you have your cuffs?"

"Yeah." She pulled a pair of handcuffs from the pocket of her jeans and stood. She yanked Yang, who was still drawing ragged breaths, around and cuffed his hands behind his back. "Keep this bastard in front of us," she gritted.

Moving cautiously, they came to a clearing where several paved walkways intersected and saw a dark figure standing over a shapeless lump on the ground. The figure turned at their approach and waved.

"It's all clear," said Archie Wolf.

As they drew nearer, they could see a man dressed in dark clothing lying face down and motionless at Wolf's feet. A rifle with a telescopic sight lay next to him.

From the direction of Princeton Avenue sirens wailed, and soon they were joined by four uniformed cops with flashlights.

When they rolled the dead man onto his back, Krystal gave an involuntary start. It was Kim Stevens, Grigory Pushkin's boss at the bank.

CHAPTER 33

Captain Abel Curry vacillated between irritation and relief but managed an even mien in front of the people assembled in his office. He did scowl at Wolf, who sat expressionless beside him at the table. Everyone was there, including DeLorenzo and Salinger. Strachey was twiddling an unlit cigar between his fingers struggling not to grin. Beside him, Krystal fidgeted in her seat. The feebies made her uncomfortable.

"The floor is yours, Mr. Strachey," said Curry. "You seem to have had all the answers."

Ignoring Curry's churlishness, Strachey smiled. "We did a little digging for our client and concluded that he was not a murderer. Had he wished to do harm to his brother, he would have done it long ago. And if Padruig Nessmith was not the murderer we could see no reason for the deaths of his brother and sister-in-law unless they were secondary victims, in the wrong place at the wrong time, leading us to believe that Grigory Pushkin was the primary victim." He turned to look at DeLorenzo and Salinger, who remained expressionless. "And that's what you thought, too, but you were willing to see an innocent man suffer to cover it up."

He turned back to Curry. "This suspicion led to everything else, and Raymond Yang's irate phone call to Pushkin before he was murdered made Yang a person of interest, as you folks would say. The rest you know."

"Not entirely," said Salinger in a mild voice, a voice that suggested he knew something that meant trouble for Strachey. "How, for example, did you confirm Yang's guilt?"

"Ah," said Strachey, studying the cigar in his hand, "that's a long story. That he was involved in the murders is a fact established by his own confession. As for his other crimes, I'm surprised the FBI did not come to the same conclusion. You had all the evidence, after all, but you ignored it."

"That is the point, Mr. Strachey," continued Salinger, warming to the subject. "Would you address the question of 'evidence,' please?"

"I think you already know," said Strachey. "The thumb drive contained everything you needed to come to the same conclusion as we."

Salinger grew solemn, "And the thumb drive contained protected bank information which you obtained illegally. Yang might not be convicted because you trapped him with fruit of the poison tree. All the evidence will be thrown out of court." For some reason, the idea seemed to please him.

"Oh, maybe," said Strachey with complete nonchalance. "We already discussed this. I'm sure the bank will now thoroughly check its books and confirm the fraud. Maybe they'll succeed in keeping it quiet; maybe they'll bring charges against Yang. I don't really care. It wasn't my money. On the other hand, Yang has already confessed to conspiracy to murder my partner here." He waved his cigar at Krystal. "Even if he can't be convicted of bank fraud, he'll do time for that. And, of course, Yang was anxious to tell us that it was his partner in crime, Stevens, who murdered all those people and took a pot-shot at Natasha Pushkin. From the beginning, this case was about the murders. Finding the bank fraud was just icing on the cake."

According to what Wolf leaked to them after Yang was interrogated, the original plan was for Stevens to ambush Pushkin on the path around the pond. But Pushkin was a moving target on his bicycle, and Stevens managed only to squeeze off a non-lethal shot to the man's back. Pushkin somehow managed to stay on his bike and disappeared around a sharp bend with Stevens close behind. He was surprised to run into the Nessmiths sitting around a picnic blanket on the verge of the pond. Pushkin had finally fallen from his bike a little further on, and Stevens made a snap decision to eliminate the witnesses. He dispatched the Nessmiths who were frozen by shock and ran to where Pushkin lay on the ground and finished him off. Fearful the noise would attract more people he ran the short distance to the parking lot and sped away in his car."

Strachey continued, "And I'm not so sure about your fruit of the poison tree stuff, either, Special Agent Salinger. Yes, we used bank information, but it we did nothing illegal to get it. In fact, Pushkin's wife handed it over voluntarily. It's no different than if a reporter got hold of it and made it public, like the Pentagon Papers. But, as I said, the fraud is small change compared to the murders, even if it is a hundred million dollars. They're two entirely separate matters. That's something for the courts to figure out. The important thing for us is that our client has been cleared of all charges. That's what we were hired to do."

Curry grunted, and with a glint in his eye turned to his sergeant. "Wolf, what do you have to say for yourself?"

"Well, sir," said Wolf, "Ms. Murphy here called me the night of the Freedom Park incident to ask for help.

As a former cop, she thought it was appropriate for a member of the force to be there in case an arrest was needed. When all the shooting started, I happened to be in the right place at the right time."

Curry was obviously dubious of Wolf's story. "And you didn't think to call me?"

Wolf managed to look sheepish. "Well, sir," he said, "this was a bank case we hadn't heard about before. I thought it best to check it out before disturbing you. I had no idea there was a connection to the other case."

Curry directed a long stare at his sergeant who steadily returned his gaze. Giving up, the Captain said, "OK, Wolf. We'll have a chat about this later." He turned to DeLorenzo and Salinger. "Do you gentlemen have anything to add?"

The two Feds exchanged a glance before Salinger spoke. "We'll take all this into consideration, Captain Curry. In the end, it's up to the court to decide. Thank you for your cooperation."

The two rose from the table, DeLorenzo favoring Strachey with a sullen stare, and left.

Strachey and Krystal stood, too. "Well," he said, "I think that about covers it. I assume we'll be called to testify at Yang's trial, and you can count on us."

Curry scowled them out the door.

Under normal circumstances, Strachey would have invited Krystal out for a celebratory drink. Instead, they drove to his house where Amy would have lunch waiting.

"Do you think everything will hold water?" asked Krystal. She had some doubts about Strachey's legal acumen.

"The court case? Hell, I don't know, and I don't really care. It's out of our hands now. The important thing for us, and for PSI, is that Padruig Nessmith is free and clear. Like I said, that's what we were hired to do."

CHAPTER 34

As the crowd swirled around her, the events of the past few weeks rolled over in Krystal's mind like a film on a never-ending loop. She was frightened by her own self-analysis. The only way she could exorcise her demons was to act. Whether she should seek professional help, as Amy Strachey had gently suggested, was a decision to be postponed. There was something she needed to do first.

Not every moment since Padruig Nessmith had been cleared of all charges had been so difficult or fraught with tension. Strachey had been pleased when Padruig's attorney, Matthew Holmes, had stopped by the office to present him with a check for their services. The amount was even more generous than Strachey had billed, and Holmes said his client wanted to express his gratitude for the physical danger they had undergone. In turn, Strachey gave Krystal an equally generous bonus which she realized was a way of salving his conscience but which he insisted was her just due for nearly being killed.

Padruig Nessmith's generosity was not limited to their fee. A week earlier she and Strachey received written invitations to Saturday lunch at the Nessmith residence. The invitation aroused a great deal of curiosity around the office. Though neither of them had a great desire to renew their acquaintance with the gloomy recluse, they felt obligated to accept.

Gavenia greeted them at the door, and there was something different about her. She still wore a long dress that covered her ankles, but instead of mourning black it was an iridescent blue, and Krystal noticed for the first time that she had blue eyes unlike her brother's nearly black ones. There may even have been a hint of rouge on her cheeks, but most startling was the smile on her face when she greeted them.

"Please, come in," she said enthusiastically. "We're very pleased you came."

She led them to the room where Krystal had pictured Padruig as a bat hanging from the ceiling. This time, the curtains were not drawn across the tall windows, which allowed light to flood inside. The antique furniture that before had appeared dull and drab, shone in the light in mellow tones of fine wood and bright, silken upholstery. There was an unmistakable lightness to the atmosphere that had been entirely absent before.

"Padruig, our guests have arrived," announced Gavenia.

Krystal had been so absorbed in the room's transformation that she had missed Padruig sitting in a corner at a low table across from a little girl of about ten or eleven with blond hair that fell in curls around her shoulders. Between them on the table was a checkerboard.

Padruig stood and came to greet them. He wore the same dark clothing, but his perpetually dour expression had been replaced by an actual smile, or as close as he could get to a smile. Krystal suspected all his clothes were dark and that his normally stern expression had been set for so long it would take a long time for the proper muscles for a smile to regain their elasticity. Once again, he reminded her of Ebenezer Scrooge, but on this occasion the Ebenezer Scrooge of

Christmas morning.

"Thank you for coming," said Padruig, his voice still low and raspy but with none of the old hostility. "I wanted to see you again to thank you personally for all you did for me." He cast his eyes toward the little girl who was still seated at the table studying the checkerboard. Padruig called to her. "Won't you come over here, dear, and meet our guests?"

The girl stood and came to them. She wore a robin's egg blue dress and white shoes. "Hello," she said.

Gavenia said, "This is Caitlin, our niece. She will be living with us from now on." Gavenia beamed at the little girl who smiled shyly at them.

So, thought Krystal, *this is the daughter of Jaidon and Christanna.* The girl had been in the custody of Child Services after her parents were murdered and must have been handed over to Padruig and Gavenia as soon as Padruig was cleared. They were her only relatives.

They enjoyed a pleasant lunch and said their good-byes, with Padruig insisting on vigorously shaking each of their hands at the door.

In the car, Strachey said, "That little girl is going to change the lives of those two. They're both smitten with her."

"I think you're right," replied Krystal. "I wonder if Padruig's main concern all along was for little Caitlin. I'm sure she's brightened Gavenia's life. She has no children of her own, and I suspect she'll spoil Caitlin rotten."

Strachey smiled. "It will be like being raised by doting grandparents."

"She must remind Padruig of Christanna," said Krystal, "the love of his life. I hope she will comfort him, bring him out of his shell."

She was reminded of Padruig and Christanna's ill-fated romance as boarding for her flight to Miami was announced. She heaved her bag over her shoulder and joined the queue, hoping she had made the right decision.

THE END

Afterword

Charlotte, North Carolina, is a main character in this book. It is one of my favorite cities, not least because I have dear friends there, and I would feel remiss if I didn't say a few words about it.

After smallpox wiped out the Catawba tribe in 18th century, a wave of Scots-Irish immigration dominated the southern Piedmont region, and from a few primitive log buildings at a crossroads in the forest, in 1755, Charlotte became the "Queen City," named after German princess Charlotte of Mecklenburg who was the Queen Consort of Great Britain and Ireland. Today the city prospers as a major financial center with the second-most banking assets after New York City.

Charlotte is now the most populous city in North Carolina and continues to grow. There are professional football and basketball teams, NASCAR racing, a major professional golf tournament, a ballet company, and a symphony orchestra.

With all its sophistication one still hears a soft "y'all" sprinkled in conversation, yet while the old families and traditions remain, they are slowly being supplanted by newcomers attracted by the business opportunities and employment, and the Southern charm of the city might be fading just a bit in the face of this onslaught of modern day carpetbaggers.

Michael R. Davidson

Acknowledgements

I owe a great debt of gratitude to two great writers: Jake Needham and Brendan DuBois.

Brendan literally out of the blue kindly offered to read the original manuscript and promptly suggested I cut a significant amount of verbiage. His advice? "Let the characters tell the story, let your characters carry the story along."

Now, Brendan is an accomplished, bestselling author with hundreds of published works. He's written science fiction, mysteries, and is a collaborator of James Patterson. Believe me, I paid attention to what he said and cut several thousand words from the original text of this book, as well as change its original title.

Brendan feared I might take umbrage at his criticism of my hallowed words. I did not, and I think the changes made for a better, more engaging story.

Jake reviewed the manuscript, too, and suggested I do a bit more proof-reading, advice I took immediately, which greatly improved the story. Jake has been a friend for a long time and his advice is always wise and well-received.

My high-school classmate, Judy Williams also offered generously of her time between globe encircling trips to proof the manuscript and thank Heaven she did. Thank you, Judy.

I also want to thank my former business partner, Hilary Coman, who is a proud Charlotte native, for introducing me to her city and sharing her knowledge of banking practices.

Michael R. Davidson